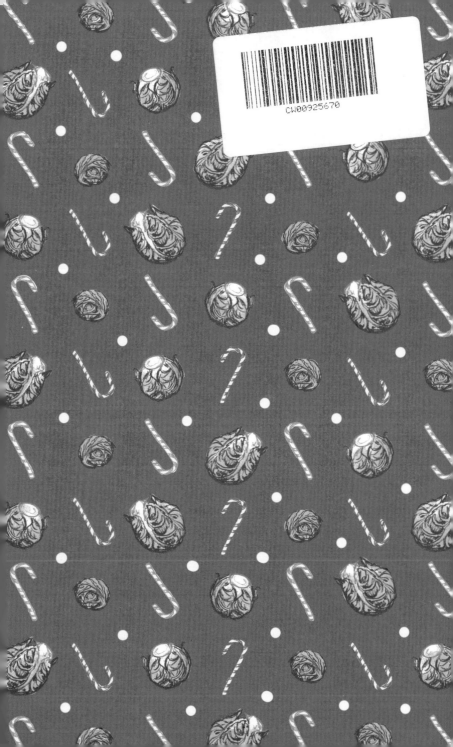

Praise for Sibéal Pounder

'Sibéal Pounder's stories fizz with fun and energy, and her characters grow more appealing with each book'
Lovereading4kids

'Madcap fun with wonderful characters [and] a touch of magic, friendship and mayhem'
Parents in Touch

'Sibéal Pounder's books are the most fought over in our house. They've brought so much joy and laughter'
Sophie Anderson, author of *The House with Chicken Legs*

'Zany, funny and irrepressibly bright'
BookTrust

'The inside of Sibéal Pounder's head must be a spectacular place! A bonkersly brilliant imagination!'
Lesley Parr, author of *The Valley of Lost Secrets*

Books by Sibéal Pounder

Sprouts

Tinsel: The Girls Who Invented Christmas

Neon's Secret UNIverse

Neon and the Unicorn Hunters

Bad Mermaids

Bad Mermaids: On the Rocks

Bad Mermaids: On Thin Ice

Bad Mermaids Meet the Sushi Sisters

Bad Mermaids Meet the Witches (for World Book Day)

Witch Wars

Witch Switch

Witch Watch

Witch Glitch

Witch Snitch

Witch Tricks

Beyond Platform 13 (with Eva Ibbotson)

Wonka (inspired by Roald Dahl)

SPROUTS

SIBÉAL POUNDER

BLOOMSBURY
CHILDREN'S BOOKS
LONDON   OXFORD   NEW YORK   NEW DELHI   SYDNEY

BLOOMSBURY CHILDREN'S BOOKS
Bloomsbury Publishing Plc
50 Bedford Square, London WC1B 3DP, UK
29 Earlsfort Terrace, Dublin 2, Ireland

BLOOMSBURY, BLOOMSBURY CHILDREN'S BOOKS and the
Diana logo are trademarks of Bloomsbury Publishing Plc

First published in Great Britain in 2024 by Bloomsbury Publishing Plc

A catalogue record for this book is available from the British Library

ISBN: HB: 978-1-5266-3946-2; eBook: 978-1-5266-3947-9;
ePDF: 978-1-5266-3943-1

2 4 6 8 10 9 7 5 3 1

Typeset by RefineCatch Limited, Bungay, Suffolk
Printed and bound in Great Britain by
CPI Group (UK) Ltd, Croydon CR0 4YY

MIX
Paper | Supporting
responsible forestry
FSC® C171272

To find out more about our authors and books visit www.bloomsbury.
com and sign up for our newsletters

For James x

Prologue

THE KRAMPUS CODE

RULE ONE: SPROUT-FLAVOURED CANDY CANES

Children MUST eat one sprout-flavoured candy cane every day. That's 365 sprout-flavoured candy canes a year, or 10,950 by the age of thirty, when the rule changes and you have to eat ten a day.

As the saying goes, a sprout cane a day keeps the witches away! The more sprout canes you eat, the less likely it is that a witch will be able to sniff you out.

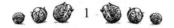

* * *

A long time ago, Santa Claus rose to power. His first act was to declare it would be CHRISTMAS EVERY DAY! The names of cities and streets were changed to more festive alternatives. Houses were demolished and built in festive shapes and from festive materials. Humbug, formerly London, became the Christmas capital of the world.

And since then everything has been very jolly indeed.

Santa's second act when he became ruler of the world was to banish the witches. They were sent away for the very simple reason that they HATE CHRISTMAS. They would destroy it if they could.

Witches have been banished to the Mince Pie Isles for many centuries now. Banishment was the only option, as they possess a book of spells so sprout-filled and powerful, it keeps them alive. Destroy the book and you destroy the witches.

The witches keep the book hidden and assign it a

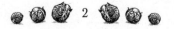

special witch guardian, who pledges to guard it with her life. It only changes hands when the guardian is too frail to protect it any more. No human has ever seen the book – or if they have, they haven't told a soul.

We know it must be somewhere out there on the Mince Pie Isles. It is a dreadful and dark place, with sprout-green-coloured caves and never-ending blizzards. There, witches lurk around every corner, on the hunt for human prey.

That's why Santa's third act was to create the Krampus Alliance, to protect us from the witches.

Do you know they eat children? Grisly things, the witches.

So eat up those sprouty candy canes!

Chapter 1

Tinselcat

In the year 4024, there lived a young girl with jet-black hair who truly hated witches.

Unfortunately, she was one.

Gryla had always *hated* being a witch. Every night before she went to bed she wished she wasn't one, and every morning when she woke up too.

Annoyingly, as a witch you could make all sorts of magic happen, but you couldn't make yourself *not a witch* any more.

She was destined to spend every second of her life on

the Mince Pie Isles, celebrating Christmas only once a year, when out there in the rest of the world it was CHRISTMAS EVERY DAY!

She'd heard stories of never-ending presents whipped up by holographic elves, of constant Christmas cheer and everyone travelling by flying sleigh! Gingerbread houses! Constantly twinkling Christmas trees and candy canes in every flavour you could imagine!

Witches believed that to celebrate Christmas every day was to rob it of its magic. *Too much of something is as good as having none of it at all*, they always said.

Gryla Garland didn't agree. And so every night, she sat on the shore, looking at the horizon and dreaming of a better, festive life.

On one such night – Christmas Eve, as it happened – Gryla spotted a strange, cloaked figure walking by the water's edge. Bent double and clearly very old, she watched as the figure hobbled closer and closer until she was standing over her.

Slowly, she lifted her hood.

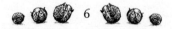

Gryla knew every witch on the island. She'd never seen this one before. Her hair was so white, it glowed.

She stared at Gryla, her eyes cloudy, frosted over as if they were made of ice.

Then she winked.

'For you,' she rasped, and she pulled from her cloak the strangest cat Gryla had ever seen.

It wriggled free of the witch's grasp and leaped into Gryla's lap. It had a tail and ears and all the bits you'd expect a cat to have. But its fur was made entirely of tinsel!

'For me?' Gryla whispered.

'For you,' the old witch nodded. 'Take care of him, but never brush the fur. A Tinselcat won't ever tangle, or tell.'

Gryla looked down at the cat as it nuzzled into her.

'What do you mean by—?' Gryla began, but when she looked up, the woman was gone.

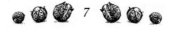

FIVE YEARS LATER

Chapter 2
Christmas Eve 4029

'Two Christmas witches!' a little witch sang. 'And a Tinselcat in a cave laaaair!'

'Gryla Garland, there will be one less witch, and one less tinsel cat in a cave lair if you don't hurry up,' her grandmother joked. She thrust a candy cane into Gryla's hand. 'Come on, we have an important spell to brew.' Then she strode off at speed through the candy-cane vines, grabbing fistfuls at a time and dropping them into the large cauldron dangling on her arm.

Gryla watched her go. Her grandmother was the

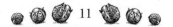

only family she had. The winters were harsh on the Mince Pie Isles and not all witches survived. She was a kind old witch, with red hair, short and spiky. She wore a simple black cloak, but had decorated it with a collar of tinsel.

All around them a blizzard whipped the snow into a frenzy and sent Gryla's long black hair flying across her face. The blizzard was always at its worst on Christmas Eve and the witches usually spent the time indoors preparing for Christmas Day. It was unusual to be picking candy canes in such weather.

A bunch of twigs hurled past and hit Gryla head-on.

'Great,' she muttered, picking one out of her dress and snagging the fabric. It was her favourite dress, shiny and multicoloured like the candy canes. She wore it every Christmas.

The candy canes were the witches' main source of food. Across the world all food had been replaced with candy canes. They came in all sorts of flavours, but not on the Mince Pie Isles. There, every candy cane, no matter the colour, always tasted of Brussels sprouts. Sprouts, sprouts, sprouts and nothing but sprouts. Sometimes, if you were lucky, you'd find one that tasted mildly of mint and heavily of sprouts.

Once a witch said she'd got a chocolate one, but no one believed her. That only happened outside the Mince Pie Isles. There you could get any flavour you wanted: chocolate flavour, mince-pie flavour, soup flavour, pizza flavour, bread flavour … It was yet another reason Gryla didn't want to be a witch.

Luckily, witches, being traditional, had managed to preserve a small crop of essential ingredients for making mince pies the old-fashioned way, from scratch. No human alive had seen a mince pie in real life, but the witches ate them every Christmas Eve. And they had *real* sprouts too – only a few ancient, shrivelled ones, but real ones nonetheless. They weren't for eating, they were used for only the most important of spells.

'Less freezing, more picking,' her grandmother called

to her. 'You know the saying: melt no candy canes, make no spells!'

'She's on edge today,' Gryla said, giving Tinselcat a weary look. 'Wonder what spell they're brewing … ? Look at us all out picking in this weather.' She gestured to the other witches in the fields, their cauldrons stuffed with candy canes. 'It must be important.'

Tinselcat blinked at her.

'I wish you could talk,' she said, before lowering her voice to a whisper and asking, 'Can you talk? You can tell me.'

Tinselcat blinked again.

'Not even a miaow?' she sighed. 'Oh it would be so nice to have a friend.'

At that, Tinselcat growled.

'Not that you're not a friend,' Gryla quickly corrected herself. 'I just mean a friend to *talk to*.'

'GRYLA! CANDY CANES! NOW!'

'Yes!' Gryla called back, and she quickened her picking.

 14

Soon, she had a big basketful, in every colour and size. Big, small, striped, glowing and even solid putrid green.

'That'll do!' her grandmother called, and together they set off, hauling their cauldrons back to the cave.

While her grandmother went to direct the incoming witches, Gryla joined a queue of picker witches lining up to have the contents of their cauldrons inspected.

As soon as she'd placed her cauldron on the ground, a young witch barged in front, knocking her sideways.

'Oi, I was first!' Gryla began, but she stopped when she saw who it was.

'Oh, sorry. Didn't see you there,' the witch said.

Cackle stood at least two feet taller than Gryla, looming over her as she boomed out every word. Her hair was spiked into three glamorous horns. Plus, she had a wart on the tip of her nose that most witches could only dream about.

She was the best young witch on the Mince Pie Isles – excellent at candy-cane picking, brilliant at broom flying. The one who was going places. Well, not actually going places, because they were banished to a relatively small island. But certainly on her way to becoming an important member of the coven. She was also by far the most popular young witch on the Mince Pie Isles.

Gryla looked at her boots and scuffed the ground. She didn't even have one friend, unless Tinselcat counted.

'Wonder what they're making with all these candy canes?' Gryla muttered, trying to strike up a conversation.

Cackle snorted. 'You're not serious?'

'Do you know?' Gryla asked as she tried to get a better look.

It was hardly obvious. At the front of the cave, witches were tipping the contents of their cauldrons on to tables, and an elder witch was hurrying about, looking the candy canes over, sniffing them, giving them a lick, and throwing the best ones into a huge bubbling cauldron.

'It looks like candy-cane soup,' Gryla said, catching sight of the mixture. Thick, creamy swirls of purple and pink and gold danced about in the cauldron, flashing green and red with every stir.

Then she saw the Brussels sprouts. Three of them, shrivelled and with crispy edges, sitting on a small table next to the cauldron. She'd seen pictures of them before, but she'd never seen one in real life. This spell must be really important.

'It's not soup,' Cackle said. 'Honestly, Gryla, if you paid attention sometimes instead of moping about talking to that Tinselcat—'

'I barely talk to him,' Gryla said defensively, scooping him into her arms. 'I only talk to him when I'm … asking him if he can … talk.'

'Well, for your information, the stuff in that cauldron is *the* potion,' Cackle said. 'You know, the one that awakens the ancient magic of Befana.'

The potion fizzed and sparked.

'Oh no,' Gryla whispered. She knew the name Befana,

the witch of Christmas, the most famous witch of all time. The one who –

'It's the potion for picking the new guardian of the Book,' Cackle said. She tipped her candy canes on to the table. 'And I think we all know it's going to be me.'

The ceremony to pick the new guardian of the Book was a horrible case of soupy roulette. On Christmas Eve in a year when the Book was ready to change hands, the witches would brew a potion to call the spirit of Befana, the witch of Christmas. Then everyone would go to bed and Befana's spirit would put the Book in one witch's stocking! And that witch had to guard it with their life until they were old and frail.

'Top-rate picking, Cackle, well done!' an elder witch said, as Cackle sauntered off.

Gryla inched forward and tipped out her candy canes. She hoped Cackle *was* going to be the next guardian. The last thing Gryla wanted was to be *the Witch* with *the Book*.

'Gryla, your pickings,' the elder witch said with a cough.

'Yes,' Gryla muttered, her eyes fixed on the potion.

'You're getting, er, better. Some good stuff here. This, however, is a twig. As is this one … aaand this one.'

Chapter 3

A Red Bauble

In a rocky tower on the farthest tip of the Mince Pie Isles, two young witches sat with their feet up. One had bright red hair and one bright pink hair and they both had matching green gowns with puffed shoulders. The pink-haired witch was using one puffed shoulder as a pillow, her eyes slowly shuttering closed as the hands on the clock inched towards midnight.

Hanging above them was a large red bauble.

They weren't just any witches, they were the bauble's newly appointed lookouts.

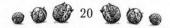

'Where'd it come from again?' the red-haired witch said, startling the other one awake.

Inside, the bauble was alive with swirls of gold and flurries of snow.

'Dunno, some witch made it, apparently,' the pink-haired witch said with a yawn, straightening up in her seat. 'It's meant to show significant things in the future. Used to get passed around children who needed hope most, but when witches got banished, they brought it here to make sure the Krampuses didn't destroy it.'

'Oooh, I wonder if it'll show us anything?' the red-haired witch said.

'It only shows a blizzard these days,' the pink-haired witch said.

'But imagine if we saw something,' the red-haired witch went on, her nose practically touching it now. 'Especially with the ceremony happening tonight. Now the Book is being brought out of hiding, it'd be the perfect time to steal it.'

'You know, my gran did the lookout job when she was

younger too,' said the pink-haired witch. 'She said she was told to look for Krampuses on ceremony night, but she never saw anything except blizzards. I mean, how would the Krampuses know about the ceremony anyway?'

'Don't they have loads of eyes?' the red-haired witch said. 'Maybe they can see us from all the way across the sea!'

They both laughed nervously.

'Have you ever seen one, you know, in real life?' the red-haired witch asked.

'No, have you?'

'No, just heard about them. They sound grim. How did they even come to exist? Who makes such monsters?'

'It was Santa,' the pink-haired witch said gravely, sitting up in her chair. 'The one who made it Christmas every day. He was really rich and he used his extreme wealth and the magic squeezed from one poor elf to make a bunch of huge, hairy, hulking monsters, with six rows of fangs and a head covered in eyes. And that's the Krampus Alliance that exists today. They have one job: to protect the Christmas world at all costs.'

'How did he come up with that idea?' the red-haired witch mused.

'They say he'd read about a man called Mr Krampus in the history books, a fearsome character with a cane carved with a thousand eyes,' the pink-haired witch explained. 'The cane was supposed to be all-seeing, and that's what Santa wanted his Krampuses to be – all-seeing, all-knowing. There would be Christmas cheer every day, and if a Krampus caught you behaving out of step, maybe taking a day off from decorating your Christmas tree, or giving someone a kiss without mistletoe, there would be consequences. Big-fanged Krampus consequences.'

The red-haired witch gulped. 'I hope we don't see one in the bauble.'

'Nah,' the pink-haired witch said as she shoved a mince pie in her mouth. 'Like I said, it only ever shows a blizzard.'

'You don't think they're just pretending this bauble is magic?' the red-haired witch asked. 'Maybe they're making us sit watching it instead of going to the

Christmas Eve party in the caves. They're probably trying to cut party numbers!'

As if to prove them wrong, the blizzard in the bauble began to slow.

The witches rose quickly to their feet.

Inside the bauble, the snow cleared and a figure came soaring into view, spiralling through the sky like a rocket going sideways. She was a child, with white hair decorated with gold strands of tinsel, and she wore an old soot-covered smock. She had reindeer too – real ones, not the silly holographic ones. The old kind, with beating hearts and big opinions.

'Who is it?' the red-haired witch whispered.

'Not a Krampus, at least,' the pink-haired one said.

They leaned in closer.

'What do we do now?' said the red-haired witch. 'She's not a witch, is she?'

'She's got a sleigh, so she can't be, can she?'

It was a strange sleigh – incredibly fancy, red with big wings spread wide.

'I don't understand why it's showing us this! Where is she?'

The girl was swooping down low now, cruising over a snowy land … covered in green glowing caves and candy canes.

'The Mince Pie Isles!' they both cried at once.

Chapter 4

The Smell of Sprouts

Back in the main cave, witches young and old were cramming in, all dressed in their finest. Soon they were practically piled on top of each other, like an assortment of Christmas tree decorations thrown in a box.

The whole cave was decorated with tinsel. It was plastered on every surface – ceilings, walls, even the floor. Witches believed tinsel was the mark of sister-hood, the frayed paper representing the bonds of friendship that could be tested but never broken.

A tingle of excitement danced up Gryla's spine at the thought of seeing the ceremony, mingling with the lead-heavy feeling of dread she had when she thought about the Book.

There were stories of witches littered throughout history, hiding in all sorts of places to keep it safe, their whole lives dominated and derailed by it. The Book meant everything to the coven. And whenever she'd thought about it, Gryla had been very grateful she wasn't the one who had to guard it.

'Ah, there you are, Gryla!' her grandmother called, from where the senior witches were dipping the shrivelled old sprouts in the potion. 'Come and take a look!'

'I'll stay back here, thanks!' Gryla called over.

A thick green smoke had begun to rise from the cauldron, extinguishing the excited whispers. The smell was so putrid and powerful Gryla started to gag.

'Sprouts,' the old witch brewing it said knowingly. 'It always smells of sprouts.'

Gryla spotted Cackle up at the very front. She looked

like she'd dive into the cauldron and drink the entire contents if it meant she could guard the Book.

'And by morning,' the witch went on, 'the spirit of Befana will place the Book in one lucky young witch's stocking! This book, though none of you needs reminding, protects witches, and by doing so, protects *Christmas itself*. We are the only ones in this world who keep the memory of what Christmas once was *alive*. The Christmas we love, not what they have made it. To be chosen is the ultimate honour.'

Gryla crossed her fingers behind her back and wished it wouldn't be her. Surely the spirit of Befana had some sense.

The cave was really glowing now, a putrid, vegetable green so bright it hurt Gryla's eyes to look directly at it.

'WE CALL ON THE WITCHES OF CHRISTMAS PAST!' the elder witches chanted over and over, and soon everyone was joining in.

'WE CALL ON THE WITCHES OF CHRISTMAS PAST!'

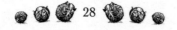

The ceiling above Gryla's head began to shake, shedding dust and small rocks that pinged off her head. She tucked Tinselcat under her arm to shield him.

'WE CALL ON THE WITCHES OF CHRISTMAS PAST!'

All around them the cave was crumbling, the green light getting brighter and brighter.

Then there was silence. The witch brewing the potion spoke alone.

'SPIRIT OF BEFANA, WE CALL ON YOU NOW TO PICK A NEW GUARDIAN. BECAUSE RUBY HERE IS VERY OLD AND SHE'S HAD ENOUGH.'

Indeed, Ruby looked wrinkly and old and like she'd very much had enough. She was barely able to hold the huge book in her arms and her frail little legs were twisted around each other like old tree roots. And though her eyes were closed, she was nodding furiously, her lips arranged into a fed-up pout.

Suddenly the Book leaped up out of the old witch's hands, making everyone gasp. Gryla watched in amazement

as it soared through the air, alive, like a tattered old bird in need of a nest. It hovered above the cauldron half open, its dog-eared pages dangling, barely clinging to its spine.

'THE BOOK OF BEFANA!' the old witch chanted. 'THE BOOK OF THE BRUSSELS SPROUT BREW! THE HISTORY OF CHRISTMAS AND US, WOVEN IN WORDS AND COOKED IN CAULDRONS!'

There was a *bang* and the roof of the cave exploded above them, sending debris and a blindingly bright green beam of light into the sky. No longer held at bay by the cave, the blizzard whipped about them.

'Great. We'll be cleaning up bits of roof all Christmas morning now,' a witch groaned.

Gryla watched in amazement as the Book dropped into the cauldron and the whole thing bubbled up and spilled over, soaking everyone's boots.

Witches carrying mince pies were flung sideways by the storm. The tinsel from the ceiling hung suspended in the air by the wind.

Tinselcat scurried up Gryla's arm and dug his claws

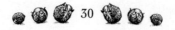

into her shoulder. He stared down at the gunk with wide eyes.

Then the old witch tipped the cauldron forward so the crowd could see what was inside.

'It's gone!' Gryla exclaimed.

The cauldron was completely empty.

'Now we wait,' the witch said with a smile. 'And tomorrow we'll find out who Befana has chosen.'

Chapter 5

A Witch Disguised as a Cook

That night, Gryla's grandmother carefully hooked a stocking over the end of Gryla's bed, then tucked her in. The little witch stared up at her cave ceiling, completely covered in tinsel, and the excitement bubbled in her belly, like it did every Christmas Eve.

Her grandmother placed Tinselcat on the bed and he nuzzled into the blanket.

'It must be magical,' Gryla sighed.

'What must be?' her grandmother asked, but she tutted

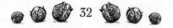

immediately, knowing Gryla too well. 'You mean if it was Christmas every day. Oh, Gryla, why would you want that?!'

'I don't know,' Gryla said. 'But it feels like there's a whole world out there and I'm not allowed to be a part of it.'

'Trust me, you wouldn't want to be,' her grandmother said. 'You know they don't eat mince pies any more? They only eat mince-pie-flavoured candy canes. Can you imagine Christmas without a real mince pie, a lovely warm one in your hand?'

'I'd give up mince pies for Christmas every day!' Gryla said.

Her grandmother smiled weakly.

'Why are you so against Christmas every day?' Gryla asked.

'Because,' her grandmother said, her face growing serious, 'having too much of something is as bad as having none of it at all.'

'Not Christmas though!' Gryla protested. 'Imagine feeling like this every time you went to bed!'

Her grandmother added an extra blanket to the bed. 'It wouldn't be exciting if it were Christmas every day. New toys every day! Children all over the world getting whatever they want, whenever they want it.'

'WHAT'S NOT TO LOVE?!' Gryla cried. 'I'm sorry, but you're old, you don't understand. Christmas every day is the best idea anyone's ever had.' She stared out of the cave window towards the horizon, blotted out by the blizzard. 'I'd give anything not to be a witch.'

'You don't mean that,' her grandmother said sadly.

'I definitely do,' Gryla whispered.

'The world may not like witches,' her grandmother said gently, 'but that's why it's so important that we do. We must fight for those who are like us, so that the world will see with time.'

'The world has moved on,' Gryla said. 'And it's so much better than this place. I hate being a witch.'

'Gryla,' her grandmother said, her tone firm now. 'Don't believe their stories. You must never forget, there are two types of tales about girls throughout history.

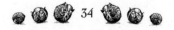 34

The ones in which girls are forgotten, and the ones in which girls are monsters.'

Gryla listened carefully.

'You mustn't trust such stories. Like the ones they tell about us witches now. Tales like that can change everything – they can become the eyes through which the world sees, until they aren't looking any more. The tales made us monsters.'

'We're not monsters?' Gryla whispered.

'No!' her grandmother said. 'And, you know, once upon a time witches lived all across the world, and they had friends who were not witches, ones who knew their secret but loved them anyway. Your great, great, great many times over grandmother was one of the most important witches in the world.'

Gryla looked up sharply, her eyes wide and interested.

'She met and helped the two girls who dreamed up delivering presents to every child. The ones behind the idea that became SANTA CLAUS.'

'Wow,' Gryla whispered.

'Uma Garland was her name. She's famous because she helped make a Brussels Sprout Brew that was used to save Christmas from the very first evil Krampus! *The* Mr Krampus, who the Krampuses of today are based on.'

Gryla shivered.

'Uma Garland lived over two thousand years ago,' her grandmother went on. 'She was born a witch, into a wealthy family in London, who lived in a fancy townhouse on Stratton Street. Only her brother and his partner knew her secret. When she became the guardian of the Book, she disguised herself as the house cook. The Book was hidden too, right there in the house, and she died an old woman of one hundred years, and no one suspected a thing. She had a *good* life. A great one, in fact. Of course, she was surrounded by kind people who protected her.'

'You mean *non-witches* protected her? They didn't hate us back then?' Gryla said, her expression one of amazement. 'We all … lived together?'

'Oh yes,' her grandmother said. 'Back then, the lies about us had not spread so far or grown so wild. But even to this day, we have friends out there.'

Gryla's mouth fell open. She couldn't imagine anyone out there liking her, let alone being her friend.

Her grandmother flicked out the light and kissed her gently on the forehead.

'Merry Christmas, sweet witch,' she whispered.

Chapter 6
Book-Shaped Stocking

Gryla sat on her bed, her knees tucked under her chin, staring at her stocking. There was a huge book-shaped bulge inside it.

'Do you see that?' she whispered to Tinselcat, but he was still snoring.

The cave was quiet and only a slither of morning light sliced through the small window. Outside, snow whipped about wildly in the wind as bits of trees and candy canes flew past.

The blizzard was picking up. Usually it settled on

Christmas morning, but for the first time ever, it was fiercer than it had been on Christmas Eve.

Tinselcat yawned and stretched his shiny paws. When he opened his eyes and saw the stocking, he yelped!

There was no getting away from the fact that the stocking was book-shaped.

'It might just be a normal book,' Gryla said hopefully. 'I'm too scared to look.'

Tinselcat nudged her. She knew what he meant. She had to check.

'Just a normal book,' she said, inching off the bed and scurrying towards it, 'that just happens to be the exact same size as the Book.' She reached in a hand and touched it, her heart beating hard.

She winced.

Even without looking, she could tell it was *the* Book. It still had some cauldron gunk on it! She shook the sprouty slime from her hand and then pulled the Book from the stocking.

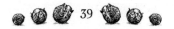

She wondered how many witches had held it.

She wondered what they'd had to do to protect it.

Slowly, she opened it and traced her fingers across the faded name scrawled on the first page: *Befana*.

'She was the witch who wrote it,' Gryla explained to Tinselcat.

Tinselcat immediately began trying to nudge the Book out of her hand, his headbutts becoming increasingly frantic.

'You think I should get rid of it?' Gryla asked hopefully. 'Why, yes, I think you're on to something.'

She flicked through the pages, unable to believe it was real. Maybe it was just a nightmare.

Her nose filled with the smell of old sprouts as she turned the pages.

You couldn't smell sprouts in nightmares.

'Oh!' she cried, spotting a spell.

Sprout and Speak

'Tinselcat,' she cried. 'It's a talking potion! It's what we've always dreamed of!'

Tinselcat began backing away.

'I suppose I could try one spell before I get rid of the Book … One quick spell.'

She was sure Tinselcat groaned.

'Wouldn't you love to talk?' she asked.

Tinselcat tipped his chin skyward, as if he was considering it.

Gryla didn't wait for an answer, after all, it's not like he could tell her anyway. She flipped the Book open and set it down on the bed.

A SPELL FOR THE TIGHT-LIPPED

Take a strand of the guardian witch's hair and a strand of hair from a tight-lipped friend. Weave them together in a tight, tight pleat and wrap it around your arm like a bracelet.

Then ask them to speak.

'Mmm hmm, right, yes, OK …' Gryla mumbled, plucking one of the hairs from her own head. 'Ow!'

Tinselcat bolted to the other side of the cave.

'Oh come on!' Gryla cried, scurrying after him. She dived to grab him, but he sprang up and began clawing his way across the tinsel-clad ceiling.

'Stop that!' she shouted as she leaped up and down trying to get a hold on him.

The tinsel decorations were collapsing all around them.

'TINSELCAT! STOP IT!'

It was raining tinsel now and the floor of the cave was covered. With nothing more to grip on to, Tinselcat fell to the ground.

'Ah ha!' Gryla cried. 'Got you!'

But he shot off again, burrowing under the newly fallen tinsel and disappearing from sight.

Gryla braced herself. 'Come out!' she said, getting on her hands and knees and feeling her way through the tinsel.

Finally, she hit something more robust.

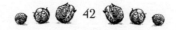

'There you are!' she cheered, pulling a miffed-looking Tinselcat from the mess.

She plucked a strand of tinsel from his back, making him hiss.

'You won't be annoyed with me in a minute,' she said excitedly, and she plonked him down and began pleating the strands together.

But something made her stop.

'Wait! Your fur – I can see …' She held it up to the window. On the little strand of tinsel she could make out words pressed into it in neat handwriting.

'You've got writing on your fur.'

She couldn't make it all out.

'Cinnamon … cherry … stir,' she said. 'Did someone write on your fur?'

Tinselcat just blinked.

She got back to pleating, weaving the strands tighter and tighter, and then wrapped it around her wrist.

'Here goes,' she said, taking a deep breath. 'Tinselcat, can you speak?'

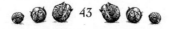

Tinselcat made a run for it.

'Oh, not this again!' Gryla cried.

'Yes! THIS again! Stop trying to make me talk!'

Tinselcat's head popped out from underneath the mass of tinsel.

'That sounded louder than usual,' he said.

They stared at each other, their eyes growing wide.

'YOU CAN TALK!' Gryla screeched.

'Oh, puddings,' Tinselcat said.

'IT WORKED!' Gryla said, scooping him up and twirling him around. Tears filled her eyes. He was her only friend in the world, her very best friend, he was so special, he was … gagging?

'What are you doing?' Gryla asked.

'Trying to undo the potion.'

'But *why*?' Gryla asked.

Tinselcat stopped. 'I'm not sure. I have an innate urge to stop this. Maybe it's because I'm a very private cat!'

Gryla beamed at him. 'Where did you come from?' she asked. 'I've always wanted to know.'

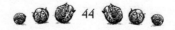

Tinselcat stared blankly at her. 'I don't remember,' he said slowly. 'I have a very faint memory of climbing a big tree. It was warm in its branches. Then a blizzard came and the next thing I remember is being here with you.'

'So you have no idea why you're made of tinsel?' Gryla said.

Tinselcat shook his head.

'I think you might come from that Christmas world out there,' Gryla said excitedly. 'And now you can talk! This is the best day ever!'

She saw the Book on the bed.

'And the worst. What should I do with the Book?'

'Beg them to take it back and give it to someone else,' Tinselcat said. 'You're a wonderful person, Gryla, but this week alone I watched you accidentally squash an entire crop of candy canes while practising your dance routine.'

'Sssh,' Gryla said, looking nervously around her room. She hadn't told anyone about that.

'And if you want my feedback on the dance routine ... ?'

'NO!' Gryla said.

'Anyway, the crop disaster was just Minceday. On Toysday you forgot to water the candy canes and they are all thumb-sized now. On Wrappingday you got lost for SEVEN HOURS on your own island! On Treesday you forgot where you left your hat and it was on your head. I could go on.'

Gryla bit her lip. 'You're right! I can't protect this book! THEY'VE GOT THE WRONG WITCH!'

And with that, she shot out of the cave and into the storm.

Chapter 7

Merrilee

'G ryla! Come back!' came Tinselcat's shouts through the wailing winds, but Gryla charged on, heading for the main cave.

'AAAAAAAAARGH!'

The blizzard was fierce, knocking her sideways until she fell over. Her hair was flying in all directions, and she could feel the gusts inflating her dress like a balloon. Snow began piling up around her like an icy prison.

'This is all very dramatic,' Tinselcat said, catching up.

'I DON'T WANT IT!' Gryla roared, throwing the

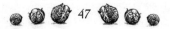

Book to the ground with all her might. It immediately bounced back up into her arms.

'STOCKINGS!' she screamed.

Witches were beginning to emerge from their caves to see what the commotion was.

'*You* got the Book? YOU!'

'Hi, Cackle,' Gryla groaned.

'NOT GRYLA!' another witch shouted.

'I really don't want it,' Gryla tried to explain. 'But it won't GO AWAY!' She threw it again and it sprang back and hit her in the face.

'Well, we're doomed,' Cackle sighed, as Gryla began wrestling the Book in the snow, grunting. 'Every witch is going to die.'

Witches were clustering around her now.

'The ghost of Befana chose Gryla Garland?' someone else cried. 'Is the ghost of Befana UNWELL?'

Gryla's grandmother came racing through the snow in her slippers and dressing gown. When she saw Gryla with the Book, she beamed with pride.

'The ghost of Befana chose wisely,' she said with a smile.

'No, I heard the ghost of Befana is unwell,' another witch said.

'Anyone but Gryla!' a witch screeched. 'PLEASE, ANYONE BUT HER!'

'Nonsense!' her grandmother said, giving the witch a furious stare.

'She doesn't even realise you *can't* throw powerful magic away!' Cackle scoffed as Gryla tried to hurl the Book into the distance again. 'Gryla, if it senses you are trying to get rid of it, it'll react and bounce back.'

Gryla chucked the Book again and it boomeranged back in her face.

'OUR LIVES ARE OVER!' a witch wailed, making the rest of the coven scream.

'I think everyone needs to calm down,' Tinselcat said, and the screaming ceased instantly.

The witches all looked down at him.

'He talks?' Cackle spluttered.

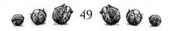

The sound of jingling bells pierced through the wind.

'POTENTIAL EMERGENCY!' came a scream from the sky, and Gryla looked up to see two witches on brooms with bells being catapulted left and right in the wind.

'Yes, we know!' Cackle said. 'Gryla got the Book!'

'NO!' the pink-haired witch cried. 'I ACTUALLY MEAN A POTENTIAL BAUBLE EMERGENCY! WE SAW SOMETHING STRANGE!'

'In the bauble?' an elder witch said, pushing to the front.

'WE WOULD LIKE TO POINT OUT TO YOU, BEFORE WE DISCUSS WHAT WE SAW IN THE BAUBLE, THAT WE HAVE FOUND A FEW FLAWS IN OUR SECURITY SYSTEM,' the red-haired witch cried.

'ONE.' The pink-haired witch was struggling to unroll a list while keeping control of her broom. 'THE BAUBLE WATCH TOWER SHOULD BE LOCATED CENTRALLY IN THE MINCE PIE ISLES, BECAUSE THEN WE COULD WARN YOU OF THINGS IN A

TIMELIER MANNER. IT'S TAKEN AGES TO FLY HERE, AND I LOST A SHOE IN THE WIND!'

'TWO,' shouted the red-haired witch. 'WE WOULD LIKE A VENDING MACHINE, ONE OF THOSE ONES WITH THE NICE WRAPPED CHOCOLATES, RESTOCKED DAILY.'

'THREE, THE CHAIRS IN THE LOOKOUT TOWER ARE NOT COMFY.'

'WHAT DID YOU SEE IN THE BAUBLE?' the elder witch snapped.

Gryla couldn't take it any more. She charged off, the Book bouncing back into her arms as she went.

'Come back!' her grandmother cried. 'It's all going to be OK!'

Gryla ignored her. She'd make for the sea. Maybe if she threw the Book in the water …

She heard a jingle.

'Slow down!' came Tinselcat's shout, and she looked back to see the little bundle of tinsel chasing after her through the snow.

There was another jingle.

'Did you hear that?' Gryla said, just as she felt something brush the back of her neck. She whipped round and caught a glimpse of red. Hoofs shot past, antlers, a puff of soot.

Gryla felt someone wrench her up, straight out of her boots!

'HELP!' she shouted, but she was too far from the coven for them to hear.

She was dropped on to the icy floor of a sleigh. Her stomach lurched as the thing surged upwards.

Frantically, Gryla scrambled to her feet and peered over the edge to look for Tinselcat. She was just in time to see the caves and candy-cane fields disappear from view.

Slowly, Gryla turned to face her captor.

Holding the reins was a young girl with white hair laced with strands of gold tinsel. She wore an old black smock covered in soot.

'What's your name?' the girl asked.

'G-ryla G-arland,' Gryla said, her voice quiet and terrified. 'Who are you?'

The girl turned and smiled at her. 'You know what? That's the first time someone's ever asked me that!'

'I don't know what you mean,' Gryla said, glancing around for an escape route. 'Where are you taking me?'

The girl flicked the reins. 'I'm Merrilee Claus,' she said. 'And I'm taking you to a world no witch has seen before.'

Chapter 8

To Humbug

It was a known fact that in 4029, everyone in the world (apart from witches) travelled by flying sleigh. Unlike the skies of yesteryear, if you looked upwards you would not see stars or birds or the occasional plane. You'd see sleighs; huge, hulking flying sleighs pulled by reindeer – some real ones, some robotic, but mostly holographic, glitching their way through the skies.

Gryla had fallen asleep somewhere between the storm and the stars and was woken with a start by the commotion around her. Above, below and at each side,

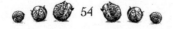

there were thousands of sleighs, bells ringing, Christmas tunes jingling. The sky was a mangle of Christmas songs playing loudly and all at once. She clutched her ears and got to her feet. They were flying high over a city of gingerbread towers dusted with snow.

'Where are we?' Gryla said with a gasp.

'Humbug, centre of the world,' Merrilee said.

'Are those giant baubles people's homes?' Gryla asked, forgetting for a moment that she was probably in very great danger.

'Yes, it's a popular part of town, near the Christmas tree forest,' Merrilee explained. 'Over there is the Gingerbread Quarter …'

The onslaught of sights and sounds was enough to make Gryla dizzy. But the blazing cheer of it all zipping past – the Santa hats! The piles of presents! The Christmas trees with twinkling lights – was everything Gryla had dreamed of and more! It was certainly *more*. Even the air smelled of cinnamon and chocolate with a hint of turkey. Everyone was dressed in Christmas outfits, from elf pyjamas to grand red ballgowns with white fur trims and everything in between.

'Now, hold on for this bit,' Merrilee said.

Gryla turned to her. 'What? Why-yyyyyyyyyyyyyy?!' she screamed too late as they plunged downwards, the sleigh spinning. Gryla gasped as she slipped and somersaulted over the front edge, landing hard on the reindeer's neck. Her fingers gripped his mane for dear life.

'HELP!' she screamed.

'I meant hold on to the sleigh,' Merrilee said with a casual roll of the eyes. 'But the reindeer will have to do.'

'We're going to hit the roof!'

Gryla couldn't watch. She squeezed her eyes shut and –

Plop.

Suddenly the Christmas jingles were a muffled hum and the air grew thick and warm. She opened her eyes. They were still moving downwards, but in total darkness, clattering against the edges of something as they went. Finally, *whoosh*! They flew out into the light and came screeching to a stop in a large, lofty gingerbread-beamed room. It was filled with parked sleighs.

Gryla fell off the reindeer and hit the ground with a thud.

'You're lucky I have real reindeer,' Merrilee said. 'You'd have fallen right through one of the holographic ones.'

'Thank you,' Gryla said to the reindeer as she got to her feet. She gave him a little pat. 'What's his name?' she asked.

'Rudolph One,' Merrilee said. 'And the other is Rudolph Two.'

Gryla shot her an amused look. 'They're both called Rudolph?'

Merrilee shrugged. 'Yeah. I heard the name once and thought it sounded classic.'

The Rudolphs held their noses in the air grandly, as if they agreed.

Gryla turned to see where they had emerged from. 'And we came down that chimney?' she said. 'Why a chimney?'

'Because that's the law,' Merrilee said. 'How do you get into your house?'

'Doors, cave holes … sometimes I jump in through a window,' Gryla said, turning in circles on her heel to look at all the fancy sleighs.

'Ah yes,' Merrilee said. 'You don't have the Krampus Anti-door Law in the Mince Pie Isles, do you?'

'The *what*?' Gryla said.

'Entry to your home must be via chimney, unless you're Santa Claus, then you can use a door, if you'd prefer,' Merrilee chimed. 'I think it's rule one thousand and five of the Krampus Code. Or maybe one thousand and six.'

'What's the Krampus Code?' Gryla asked. She plucked the Book from Merrilee's sleigh and hugged it firmly to her chest.

'The rules of law that we all have to obey,' Merrilee said. 'I've always thought it would be great to be a witch – I mean, yeah, you have to live in a cave, but you don't have Krampuses breathing down your neck.'

'I've never seen a Krampus,' Gryla whispered, which made Merrilee laugh a hollow laugh.

'Consider yourself lucky,' she said. 'I see them every day.'

She guided Gryla by the arm to a frosted window and pushed it open. The icy wind howled and stung Gryla's face. Snow-bright light flooded in. They were perched atop a snowy mountain, higher than any other building Gryla could see. Beneath them stood grand gingerbread buildings and huge bauble houses.

Merrilee pointed to the river, where tinsel-covered boats sat in mucky-looking water. It was brown and thick.

'They add chocolate,' Merrilee said. 'And the shores are either frozen like ice rinks or syrupy like a good hot chocolate. Krampus Code rule fifty-six.'

Gryla smiled. 'It sounds like a good rule.'

'You're not allowed to drink it though, rule fifty-seven. Do you see those chimneys on the other side?'

Gryla followed Merrilee's finger to the mound of

land across the river, covered in hundreds of chimneys. Coal-black ones.

'That's where the Krampuses lurk,' Merrilee said gravely. 'The chimneys are how they get in and out, but they live below the ground like devils.'

Gryla shivered.

Merrilee raised an eyebrow. 'You're not at all like he said you'd be.'

'Who?' Gryla asked.

'My friend,' Merrilee said. 'He was meant to meet us here.' She checked her watch. 'Come on, he'll be upstairs. But keep close to me. We can't have Santa discovering a witch is in his palace.'

Gryla ducked. '*Santa's* palace?'

'Don't worry, he never comes down here. He hates using chimneys. Finds them too confining.'

'Merrilee, you can't be serious? If anyone sees me … if they ask who I am … if they suspect I'm a witch –' she could feel her breath quickening – 'they'll kill me!'

'Don't worry, no one will speak to us – most people

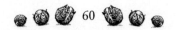

are too afraid to strike up a conversation with Santa's daughter.'

Gryla dropped the Book in shock. 'You're *Santa's daughter*?'

Merrilee chuckled. 'I keep forgetting you've been living in a cave.'

Chapter 9

A Gingerbread Throne

Gryla ducked and stayed low as she followed Merrilee through a grand corridor lined with gingerbread and iced to perfection.

'My friend is a Snowman,' Merrilee explained. 'But he can be trusted. He won't tell the other Snowmen you're here.'

'Snowmen?' Gryla said. She had heard bits and pieces about the rest of the world, but she'd never heard of Snowmen. Well, she had, but she had a feeling Merrilee wasn't talking about the kind of

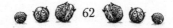

snowmen she was thinking of.

'Palace guards,' Merrilee explained. 'Distinguished by their white suits made of snow and their tall black top hats.'

'Oh,' Gryla said. 'A suit of snow must be cold.'

'It's the price you pay for potentially being the next Santa Claus.'

'Won't you be the next Santa Claus?' Gryla said. 'Being Santa's daughter.'

'Oh no,' Merrilee said. 'They wouldn't trust a girl to be Santa Claus. It's always a palace Snowman that rises up.'

Gryla followed her in silence. She could hear her grandmother scoffing at that from afar. A witch would never underestimate a girl.

'He's probably in the Throne Room with Dad. Come on, it's down here with the other main rooms,' Merrilee said.

'These aren't the main rooms?' Gryla whispered as she caught glimpses of rooms larger than all of the Mince Pie Isles caves combined.

'You know, I don't think if someone saw you they'd immediately think WITCH. For starters, you're not that scary. Do you morph into something more terrifying?'

'I beg your pardon?' Gryla said as they quickly turned a corner and were met with another long ginger-bread corridor.

'I was taught you had claws and huge jaws. How do you eat children and grind their bones with those little teeth?' She stopped and pinged one of Gryla's teeth with her finger.

Gryla glared at her.

'Unbelievable! As blunt as mine!' Merrilee said with a surprised snort.

'You don't know what witches are like at all,' Gryla said.

'I know some things,' Merrilee said. 'I know that you all hate Christmas enough to only celebrate it once a year. And I know you have a magic book that keeps you all safe … *that* book.'

Gryla hugged the Book tighter.

A little further down, Merrilee stopped abruptly at two grand double doors with mince-pie handles. She cracked her knuckles.

Through the gap in the doors where the gingerbread didn't quite meet, Gryla could see lights and the shadows of people moving around. There was a hum of voices and the air was thick with the delicious smells of Christmas – cinnamon and chocolate and piping-hot mince pies, sage and onion stuffing and freshly roasted turkey. At the far end of the room, Gryla could see a throne made of Christmas trees and covered in orna-ments.

'Feasts are always held in the Throne Room,' Merrilee whispered. 'The candy canes are the best you've ever tasted.'

She inched the doors open and reeled back. 'That's more people than I was expecting. Probably too risky to bring you in here. Oh, I know! We'll hide under the banquet table.'

'But—'

'On the count of three, run and dive. The floor is an ice rink, so we'll slide right under the table. Got it? ONE, TWO, THREE!'

And before Gryla had time to think, she felt Merrilee's arm yank her and she toppled forwards on to her stomach, the Book underneath her. She was sliding fast! She caught a quick glimpse of gowns in reds and greens and golds, and then high shoes with candy-cane striped heels and hundreds of big black boots as they skidded underneath the tablecloth.

The chatter was loud. Gryla could hear laughter and crunching candy canes, the sound of glasses clinking.

'I don't see Klaus,' Merrilee said.

'Merrilee,' came a sudden hiss, and Gryla jumped in fright. She turned expecting to see the Snowman they were looking for, but instead she came face to face with a small holographic elf grinning madly.

'Argh!' Gryla screamed, leaping up and smacking her head on the table.

66

There was a creak, and a groan, and then an almighty crash!

Silence descended. Then came a crunch from the end of the table. A boot on the floor.

'MERRILEE?' came a jolly bellow. 'IS THAT YOU UNDER THERE? I bet it's Merrilee.'

Chapter 10

One Holographic Elf

'Fred!' Merrilee hissed. 'You are in so much trouble. Why did you have to scare her like that!'

The elf sighed. 'In my defence,' he said, his face glitching and making his nose temporarily invisible, 'I need to make a toy *now*. What do you want?'

'It's not a good time,' Merrilee said. 'Unless you can stop Santa looking under this tablecloth somehow?'

'No,' the elf said. 'I'm only really programmed to provide *stuff* as requested. I'm not really sentient enough to problem-solve.'

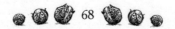

Merrilee put her head in her hands.

'So what will it be?' the elf asked.

The sound of belled boots grew closer.

'Just … some … Christmas sunglasses?'

With a little *pop* and a puff of smoke, the elf produced two ridiculous pairs of sunglasses decorated with festive lights and pompoms.

Then he vanished.

At that exact moment, the tablecloth was pulled up. Thinking quickly, Merrilee jumped out, shielding Gryla from view.

'Oh, HI, DAD,' she said, making sure the lace tablecloth fell down behind her.

Through a small gap in the lace, Gryla could see a red-cheeked man with a bushy white beard.

Santa.

'My darling daughter,' Santa said to Merrilee.

'Your Greatness,' she replied with a bow of the head. 'Your Highest Santa-ness.'

'She's not what you'd expect,' Gryla heard someone

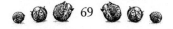

murmur. 'She doesn't dress like the daughter of Santa. Look at the soot on her!'

'It's lucky they don't let girls inherit the throne,' another said with a snort.

'And I thought *I* was meant to be the one covered in soot! Ho ho ho!' Merrilee's father said.

Gryla saw Merrilee wince. Clearly, she hated the 'ho ho ho'.

'You've never been covered in soot,' Merrilee said. 'Just the finest red silk and a gleaming white trim. Your boots wouldn't know what soot was if you kicked them up an ancient chimney!'

At that the crowd gasped, and Santa jolted in surprise.

'You'll have to excuse my daughter,' he said. 'She's a bit of a purist. Thinks Santa should know his way around a chimney!'

At that, the crowd erupted into hysterical laughter.

Gryla watched Merrilee with fascination. In her soot-covered smock – among all the glitz and glamour in the centre of the world – she looked defiant.

'I could overlook your dislike of chimneys if you'd just get rid of the Krampus Alliance,' she said.

An uneasiness swept the room like a cold wind. Everyone awkwardly turned and continued their conversations.

'But they keep us safe, ho ho ho!' Santa said quickly. 'And they keep Christmas jolly.'

'They do not,' Merrilee protested. 'Their punishments are extreme – and they punish little children.'

'Only naughty children,' Santa said, with an awkward glance at the crowd. He lowered his voice to a whisper. 'Merrilee, the Krampus Alliance is here to protect you and it's not a good idea to question them. Please, remember your poor mother. The Krampuses are a little heavy-handed, but without them the witches would grind your bones.'

'How do you know that? Have you ever spoken to a witch?' Merrilee asked.

Santa looked confused. 'Of course I haven't. They were banished to the Mince Pie Isles centuries ago, and that is where they will stay. Ho ho ho.'

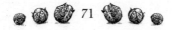

'Stop throwing in an unnecessary "ho ho ho",' Merrilee winced.

'Sorry,' Santa muttered. 'It's a habit.'

'Where's Klaus?' Merrilee asked.

'I sent him on an errand. To Nutcracker Parade, to get more of those candy canes that crackle and fizz when you chew them!'

The crowd cheered.

'Won't you stay and have some candy canes with us?' her dad said.

'Maybe another time,' Merrilee said. And with that she grabbed two fistfuls of candy canes and raised them high in the air. 'Merry Christmas!' she shouted, before kicking open the doors and storming off.

'Err,' Gryla said as she sat stuck under the table.

'CHILDREN!' Santa said with an awkward chuckle. 'I'll never understand them. Now, shall we have a dance?'

A Christmas jingle started up and the crowd began to twirl.

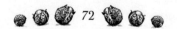 72

'Well, come on,' came a voice in Gryla's ear. She turned to find Merrilee an inch from her face.

'ARGH!'

Before she could hit her head again, Merrilee pulled her out from under the table and they charged down the hall.

'I thought you'd forgotten me!' Gryla cried as she tore after her … friend? (*Was* she a friend?)

'Klaus won't be back for a while. Come on, we'll hide you in my room.'

Chapter 11

Before Midnight

As they raced along the corridor to Merrilee's bedroom, the palace grew grander. The windows multiplied, the icing that decorated the walls spread out like snowflakes, and the ceilings rose up until the twinkling lights strung across them looked like distant constellations.

'This one is mine,' Merrilee said, heaving open a heavy door and flicking the light on.

Gryla dropped the Book in shock. Her eyes darted about, unsure what to look at first.

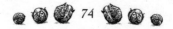

The walls were covered in a beautiful holly wallpaper, the berries glowing. A round window framed the magical Christmas city beyond, the snow falling thick and fast and making the view look like Merrilee's own giant snow globe. The bed was a whopping Christmas stocking! It was woven in thick golden threads and suspended in the air. Gryla ran around the room, spinning and marvelling at every detail. There was a candy-cane dispenser, filled with every flavour of candy cane you could dream of. There were bookcases, taller than trees and crammed with Christmas books. A big projector was showing an ancient Christmas film.

'That film was released in the year 1990,' Merrilee said, making Gryla gasp.

'I have access to an archive of every Christmas film ever made,' Merrilee said.

The en suite had a chocolate shower! The toilet sang Christmas songs!

Back in the room, Gryla noticed a green plinth in the corner. On it was carved: *FRED, ELF OF MERRILEE*

CLAUS OF HUMBUG. Beneath it was a little counter that read: *5 Christmas toy wishes granted.*

'Only five?' Gryla asked. 'Is he new?'

'Oh, I never really use him. Fred finds me infuriating, he has toy-making targets to hit every month. Nothing feels exciting when you can have whatever you want whenever you want.'

Gryla stared around the room. She couldn't imagine being bored when so festively *rich*. Merrilee lived in a dream.

'What do you want to do first?' Merrilee asked.

That evening, Gryla danced around in the chocolate shower, laughing hysterically as the toilet gurgled Christmas tunes. She leafed through Christmas books, marvelling at all the stories long forgotten. Then Fred magicked her up a pair of replacement boots, since hers were stuck in the snow on the Mince Pie Isles.

They watched Christmas films, laughing and crying together, while the candy-cane machine dispensed an edible feast on to their laps, each one a new, delicious flavour Gryla had spent her life dreaming of tasting. She munched on crumbly gingerbread flavours and smooth chocolate ones, and some that tasted like crisp roast potatoes, turkey and gravy. She tried novelty soot-flavoured ones and others that made your stomach feel like you were falling down a chimney. She even dared to lick a limited edition Krampus-flavoured one, which tasted like mould and made her feel sick.

They tried on Santa's spare beards and old suits and danced around the room to Christmas tunes from the twentieth century. They decorated the Christmas tree with regal baubles and ribbons, then they climbed into Merrilee's giant stocking bed and she pulled a thread, hoisting them higher and higher. Just when Gryla thought they couldn't go any further, the turreted roof swirled open and the stocking rose up into the snowy sky.

The grand city glistened in the moonlight beneath them.

'Wow,' Gryla whispered. She had never been

77

somewhere so beautiful. It was lights and baubles and tinsel galore.

Tinsel.

It made her think of Tinselcat. She hoped he was all right without her. She tried to comfort herself with the fact the other witches would look after him – and now that he could talk, he'd be perfectly capable of letting them know exactly what he needed.

'Ah,' Merrilee said, snuggling up next to Gryla and handing her some binoculars. 'Look down there, where the bridge meets the north side of the river.'

Gryla peered through the binoculars. It was a sweet sight that made her smile. Two young children were playing, their knees deep in snow. They had a green ball that they were throwing to each other.

'That's lovely,' Gryla smiled, trying to hand the binoculars back. But Merrilee's face was serious.

'Keep looking,' she said.

When Gryla looked again, the boys had stopped playing. The ball was nowhere to be seen. She shifted

her gaze to the left and recoiled in horror. Standing before the boys was a Krampus, huge and hairy, fangs lathered in gloopy spit. In its mouth was the ball. Its eyes were fixed on the boys. They were shaking and holding on to each other for dear life. The Krampus bit down, bursting the ball before spitting it out.

'Krampus Code rule four thousand and ninety-six,' Merrilee said. 'Only festive games are acceptable. These include: snowball fights, fastest snowman-building and board games that cause arguments.'

Gryla kept watching. The Krampus wasn't finished with them yet. He marched the boys into town, towards the little bauble houses, snarling and snapping at their necks to make them move faster.

When they reached the boys' house, a couple emerged from inside and began to sob, grabbing the children and hugging them tightly.

The Krampus rose up off the ground, his claws raised, and then with an almighty *bang* he came crashing down on the bauble house, smashing it to pieces!

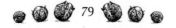

'He just destroyed their house!'

The family huddled in the cold together as the Krampus stalked off.

'Well,' Merrilee said. 'That's what you get for doing an awful thing like playing a game that isn't considered festive.'

Gryla sat with her mouth open, unable to believe it.

'That's cruel,' she finally said.

'That's why I brought you here,' Merrilee said. 'You're going to help me destroy the Krampuses once and for all.'

'WHAT?' Gryla cried.

'We're going to change this whole out-of-control Christmas world – together.'

'How?' Gryla cried.

Merrilee just smiled.

'But what if … I quite like this out-of-control Christmas world?' Gryla said quietly.

'You'll quickly get sick of it, trust me,' Merrilee said. 'Do you think everyone *likes* decorating their Christmas tree *every morning*, or listening to constant Christmas jingles, or feeling the pressure to constantly request toys so the Krampus doesn't pay you a visit? It's nice for a few days, but it quickly becomes a nightmare. And just think, Gryla,' Merrilee went on excitedly, 'if we rid the world of the Krampuses and their ridiculous festive rules, everyone will be free. Even the witches.'

Gryla's eyes lit up.

'It is, after all, the Krampus Code that keeps the witches on the Mince Pie Isles. What the Krampuses have created is a prison – for everyone. Christmas hasn't been jolly for a long time. Help me fix it.'

Gryla watched through the binoculars as the family tried to pull what remained of their possessions from the rubble.

'My mum was against the Krampuses,' Merrilee said quietly. 'She saw what they were doing and she wanted my dad to stop them. But the Krampuses got to her first. They say she froze to death after a fall in the palace gardens, but I know it was them. She was too powerful and they had to get rid of her. From that day on I vowed to finish what she started. But for that, I need you.'

'Merrilee, that's awful. I'm so sorry …' Gryla paused. Merrilee really had no idea what kind of witch Gryla was. She thought back to Tinselcat's list of her many mistakes, the witches bemoaning the fact that she was the one who got the Book. Merrilee had gone to so much trouble and put herself in real danger to capture her.

Gryla cleared her throat. 'May I ask you one thing?' she said quietly.

'Sure.' Merrilee smiled.

'What makes you think I can defeat the Krampuses?'

But Merrilee was distracted. 'He's back!' she said, pointing madly at a lone figure flying a grand red sleigh through the sky.

Before Gryla could get a good look, Merrilee pulled a thread on the stocking, making it plummet back down to the ground.

'Come on!' she said excitedly as she slipped out from

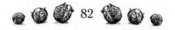

the huge stocking and ran to the door. 'He's going to be thrilled to meet you!'

They tore down the dark corridor and through the door to the sleigh garage. Gryla froze. She could make out the outline of a man in the shadows, tall and cold.

'We've been waiting for hours!' Merrilee said, barrelling into him and sending him flying. His hat rolled across the floor and landed at Gryla's feet.

She could see now that the hat made up most of his height. He wasn't tall at all. He was only a boy, around their age.

His suit was perfectly crafted out of snow. It shed snowflakes as he bent down to pick up his hat.

'You actually did it,' he said in amazement.

'Of course,' Merrilee said, pointing at the Book. 'One witch with a book, as requested.'

Chapter 12

Klaus

Merrilee put the sunglasses her elf had made on Rudolph One and Rudolph Two.

Gryla had never seen a disgruntled reindeer before, but she was certain she'd seen two of them now.

'This is Klaus,' Merrilee said. 'The most senior palace Snowman, and the only person I trust in this whole cold place, aside from my dad.'

He put his hat back on, but not before tipping it in Gryla's direction.

'Klaus was the one who came up with the idea of

capturing you,' Merrilee said excitedly. 'He wants to get rid of the Krampuses as much as I do, don't you, Klaus?'

'I do,' Klaus said.

Gryla noticed his eyes were fixed on the Book. She held it tighter.

'But for that we need magic, and you have magic spells aplenty in that book,' Merrilee said.

Klaus stepped forward, making Gryla step back.

'Don't worry,' he said, his eyes still on the Book.

'Klaus has been monitoring the Mince Pie Isles for years from afar, and when he spotted an excessive green glow coming from the caves, we knew it meant the ceremony was happening – the Book was choosing a new guardian. One that would be easier to catch.'

'Easier to catch?!' Gryla scoffed, though to be fair, she had been very easy to catch.

'No offence,' Merrilee said with a smile.

'I sent Merrilee,' Klaus said, 'because she is the best sleigh-rider in Humbug – the whole world, in fact. Plus,

I knew the witches would have some tricks up their sleeves and they'd be less likely to suspect a young girl. I presume you're well stocked in Krampus defences.'

Gryla thought about the candy-cane cannons they'd been testing – with mixed results. 'Definitely,' she said, keen not to give anything away.

Klaus's suit frosted at the cuff, replenishing itself.

'Is it made of real snow?' Gryla said.

'Of course,' Klaus said. 'I am a Snowman after all.'

He took off the jacket and handed it to her. Underneath he was wearing a crisp white shirt. The suit jacket was heavy but soft, cold but bearable to hold.

'The hat,' he explained, removing it from his head, 'is very important. Every Snowman is chosen at birth – a top hat is placed on the most festive baby born that day.'

'How can one baby be more festive than another?' Gryla asked.

'It's all to do with how much your cry sounds like a "HO HO HO",' Merrilee explained.

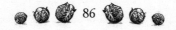

'I see,' Gryla said. The Christmas world was stranger than even she had imagined.

'After that, you're sent to a special school,' Klaus went on, 'where some Snowmen rise and others melt. The melts return home. But the ones that survive move on to the Palace. And one day, one of us will be Santa Claus.'

'There's a Snowman school?' Gryla said.

'There are loads of them, and Humbug's is the biggest in the world.' He marched to the window and pointed at a huge building made from snow with towering ice pillars. The crest on the top was two crossed carrots, each topped with a Santa hat.

'I loved it there,' Klaus said. 'I only left last year.'

'He graduated early,' Merrilee said proudly, 'and became my dad's right-hand Snowman!'

Gryla handed back the jacket and noticed her hand was dripping wet.

'It melts when it's not on a Snowman,' Klaus said. 'It means no one can impersonate us.'

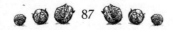 87

'So does that mean you have to wear it *all the time*?' Gryla asked.

'Yep,' Klaus said. 'But it fits nicely over my pyjamas. Now, about that book …'

Chapter 13

Extinct Elves

The trio stood in the quiet garage, all eyes on the Book.

Gryla held it tightly as Merrilee stepped closer, her face alight with hope.

'Look, Gryla, your book is our only hope for getting rid of the Krampuses. A long, long time ago, Santa borrowed an elf and he made it use its magic to make the Krampuses. And then the elf died.'

'And then *all* the elves died,' Klaus said. 'Some sort of elf plague or something, no one really knows.'

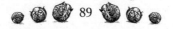

'And that was centuries ago,' Merrilee said. 'The Krampuses have been here ever since, by Santa's side, with silly festive rules and torturous punishments if you don't obey them.'

Klaus turned to her, his eyes wide. 'Shhhhhhh. They might hear you.'

'They know when you are sleeping and they know when you're awake, they know when you've been bad or good, so be good for goodness sake,' Merrilee sang sinisterly, making Gryla shiver.

Klaus reached for the Book. 'May I?' he asked.

'No.' Gryla stepped back. 'Not until I understand exactly what you want to use it for.'

'Without elf magic, witch magic is our only hope,' Merrilee said. 'Isn't that right, Klaus?'

'Uh, yeah,' he said, inching closer to Gryla.

'Real elves are gone?' Gryla said, moving back to keep the distance between them.

'Definitely,' Merrilee said. 'That's why we have those annoying holographic ones now.'

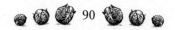 90

Klaus's eyes were still fixed on the Book. Gryla felt uneasy. She saw his fingers twitching. He was desperate for the Book.

'A witch destroyed a Krampus before,' Merrilee said. 'So we thought maybe you could do it again. Her name was Uma—'

'Garland,' Gryla said, making Merrilee look up in surprise.

'So you know the story!' Merrilee said. 'She was a huge beast of a woman who lived hundreds of years ago and only spoke in growls and lived underground. She helped two girls brew a Brussels sprout potion and they forced the Krampus to drink it. After that, he perished.'

'That's not what she was like,' Gryla said.

'How would you know?' Klaus said, and then he lunged for the Book.

It was out of Gryla's hands before she could stop him.

'Give that back!' she shouted.

The Book wriggled in Klaus's arms, but he was holding it too tightly for it to come back to her.

'It's like it's alive!' he laughed.

'Klaus,' Merrilee said sternly. 'Give it back to her and wait until she understands.'

'No.'

Klaus's face turned as cold as his suit and his eyes darkened.

'What do you mean, "No"?'

'I can't believe you fell for it,' he said, rounding on Merrilee. 'You don't understand magic at all, do you!'

Merrilee looked surprised. 'What?'

'Elf magic is the most powerful magic in the world,' Klaus said, marching arrogantly around the room, the Book struggling in his arms. 'Much more powerful than witches' magic. You can't destroy the Krampuses with this book! Only elf magic can destroy them, and the elves are all dead.'

'But you said—' Merrilee started, but Klaus cut her off.

'The only thing this book does is protect the witches,' he snarled, 'and their dangerous view that Christmas should be once a year.'

'No, no, no,' Merrilee fretted, and she raced to Gryla's side and put an arm around her.

'The only reason they've managed to resist for centuries is because of this book,' Klaus said, 'and that's why they had to be banished, not eliminated. But now that I have it, I can finally destroy the witches and stamp out the last traces of the old Christmas ways. Merrilee, you've just made me the most powerful Santa Claus the world has ever seen!'

'My *dad* is Santa Claus,' Merrilee growled. 'And he's going to be very upset with you.'

There was a huge *BANG*.

Gryla fell to the floor, her ears ringing.

'Ah,' Klaus said, consulting his watch. 'Right on time. You see, the Krampuses don't like Santa Clauses whose children try to plot their demise. Remember what happened to your mother? They've never been fans of your family. I think they'd prefer it if *I* was Santa now.'

Screams rang out from Santa's quarters.

Merrilee raced to the door.

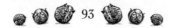

'I think your dad will just *love* the dungeons though, so I wouldn't worry,' Klaus chuckled.

'DAD!' Merrilee cried, and she flung open the door.

Standing there was a huge Krampus.

The sight of the beast up close took Gryla's breath away.

Wiry hair covered every inch of its huge body. It had fangs so sharp and shiny they glowed in the light. Its rows of eyes were rolling in its head in every direction, and the hair on its back was spiked. It growled and chomped like a wild animal.

'And these two will go to the dungeons as well,' Klaus ordered. 'The witch won't be there long though. Once I destroy this book, she'll free up some space.'

Chapter 14

Tinselclaws

Gryla and Merrilee held each other tightly as the Krampus closed in on them. Beyond the hulking creature's hairy frame, they could see Klaus making off with the Book. He got all the way to the door when a strange sound from under the sleigh made him halt.

The Krampus halted too and swivelled towards it.

They all listened.

It sounded like someone ripping ice, were such a thing possible. A long squeak and a small snap, then a few drips.

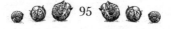

'What was that?' Klaus said, tiptoeing closer to the sleigh.

Gryla looked to Merrilee, but she just shrugged.

Klaus got down on his knees, the Book still firmly in his grasp. Cautiously, he peered underneath.

'Nothing there,' he said, a note of relief in his voice. 'Just some melting ice.'

'JUST SOME MELTING ICE?!' came a yell, and out from under the sleigh, half frozen, claws bared was …

'TINSELCAT!' Gryla yelled.

'AAAARGH!' screamed Klaus as the cat attached itself to his face. 'WHAT IS IT?'

Gryla didn't waste a second. While Tinselcat wrestled with the awful Snowman, she dodged past the Krampus and grabbed the Book from Klaus's hands.

'Miv mat mack!' Klaus tried to shout through a mouthful of ice-cold tinsel.

Merrilee dived at the Krampus, knocking him back through the door. Then she shoved a flailing Klaus

through too, grabbed Tinselcat and locked the door on both of them.

Together, Gryla and Merrilee heaved a sleigh across the door to block it.

The door shook violently as the Krampus walloped it from the other side.

'I'm so glad to see you,' Gryla said, picking up Tinselcat and giving him a hug. 'You're freezing.'

'No, I'm thawing,' he said. 'That's what happens when you spend a twenty-four-hour journey clinging to the bottom of a sleigh.'

'I can't believe this is happening,' Merrilee fretted. 'I'm so sorry, Gryla, I thought I could trust Klaus.'

Cracks began to snake up the door.

'It won't hold for much longer,' Merrilee said. 'What are we going to do?!'

Gryla climbed into Merrilee's sleigh, placing the Book down carefully.

'We've got to go,' she said, sitting Tinselcat on top of the Book. 'We haven't much time.'

'Of course,' Merrilee said sadly.

Gryla held out a hand for Merrilee. 'You can't stay. Come with us.'

'With you?' Merrilee said.

'You can't fight them alone,' Gryla said.

'But I can't leave my dad.'

'I know where we can find help,' Gryla said.

BANG.

The door was going to buckle any second.

'You heard Klaus,' Merrilee said. 'Witches are no match for Krampuses.'

'I don't mean the witches,' Gryla said. 'Come on, I can't leave you here. Trust me.'

The door gave way. The Krampus charged in.

'GET THE BOOK!' Klaus screamed.

Merrilee dived into the sleigh, and with a flick of the reins they shot off up the chimney and into the sky.

Gryla looked back to see Klaus standing at the window. His snow-white suit was shedding and turning a Santa red.

'THERE'S NOWHERE TO HIDE!' he screamed. 'THERE'S NOWHERE TO HIDE!'

'Where are we going?' Merrilee said. 'Who can possibly help us?'

'I know a thing or two about magic,' Gryla said with a smile. 'It's stubborn, and it certainly doesn't just die out.'

Merrilee gasped. 'You think the elves are alive out there somewhere, don't you?'

Gryla nodded. 'And I know just where to look.'

Chapter 15

Ho Ho Ho Ho Ho Ho Ho Ho Ho Ho Highway

Gryla and Merrilee flew through the sky to the sound of swishing sleighs and jingling bells. No one had any idea what was happening at the palace.

Something had occurred to Gryla. Something that was causing excitement to bubble in her belly. *If* they could find the elves and *if* the elves possessed more powerful magic than witch magic, then maybe – along with destroying the Krampuses – they could help Gryla as well. Maybe they could break the spell of the Book

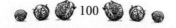

and free her from being its guardian.

'WATCH WHERE YOU'RE GOING!' someone screeched, and a sleigh shot up over their heads, narrowly missing them.

'The rules of the sky are not clear!' Gryla said.

Merrilee laughed. 'You just have to read the signs.'

The sky was alight with flashing signs, but they made no sense to Gryla. There was one with a big picture of a present and a cross through it. One with a reindeer pooing and a big cross through it. One with an elf holding tools and an arrow pointing to it. One with some jaws crunching down on a Christmas cracker. They were everywhere; above, below, left and right. One sign that kept popping up was a sleigh and three candy canes above it, then one with two candy canes above it. Up ahead in the flying lane marked with only two candy canes, there were just two rows of sleighs. The three candy-cane-signposted areas had three flying lanes.

'Ah …' Gryla said, as she worked it out. 'The candy canes represent the number of flying lanes.'

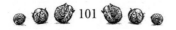

'Exactly,' Merrilee said. 'And the jaws clamping down on a cracker means a Krampus Sleigh Stop. They like to do random checks, to make sure everyone is being festive.'

'We'll avoid those then,' Gryla said as she looked over her shoulder. 'Do you think they'll come after us?'

'Definitely,' Merrilee said. 'But it'll be hard to find us in this crowd.'

Soon they reached a huge highway cutting through the snowy sky, with sleighs moving so fast they were just blurs of colour. A flashing sign showed a sleigh and *ten* candy canes.

'Ten lanes,' Gryla said with a gulp.

'The Ho Ho Ho Ho Ho Ho Ho Ho Ho Ho Highway,' Merrilee said. 'Ten Hos to represent the ten lanes. I've never been allowed to fly my sleigh here. It's the fastest sleigh route in the world.'

Just as she said it, a sleigh barged past and pinged off so fast it was a speck in seconds.

Gryla looked up at the signpost hovering over their heads. It was a list of destinations:

Gingerbread Quarter: baby's sleep (30 minutes)

New Kringles: Naughty child's sleep (2 hours)

Noelle: Try to catch Santa sleep (4 hours)

Mitten City: Early stocking opener's sleep (6 hours)

Nutcracker Parade: Perfect Christmas sleep (8 hours)

Sacktown: At risk of sleeping in sleep (9.5 hours)

Greenwreath: Possibly forgotten it's Christmas sleep (11 hours)

Old Yule: Definitely forgotten it's Christmas sleep (13 hours)

The North Pole: WARNING: BEYOND THE END OF THE LINE: 12 hours with refuelling pit stop. Then open skies North for 12 more hours

'Which one are we going to?' Merrilee asked.

Gryla smiled. 'They really don't teach you anything about the history of Christmas any more, do they?'

And with a flick of the reins, they were off.

Rudolph and Rudolph shot forward and the icy wind whipped Gryla's cheeks back with such force she thought they might hit her ears! There was so much pressure on her eyeballs she felt they might pop out the back of her head.

'AAAAAAARGH!' she screamed.

They shot past more signs, looking desperately from left to right, trying to take them in. They pelted through clouds, swooping up and down and passing billboards displaying strange adverts for Christmas gifts:

SANTA'S SOCKS EAU DE PARFUM
What better gift to give than the opportunity to smell like Santa's socks!

KRAMPUS CHOMP
Play the family game everyone's been talking about! How many tree ornaments can you remove from the Krampus's jaws before he CHOMPS?

GINGERBREAD QUARTER FOOD-LOVER'S TOUR
Treat someone this Christmas with our ultimate

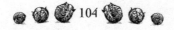

Humbug food-lover's tour. Sample the best candy canes in town, including the world-class creations at The Christmas Lunch Club.

BEARD!

Give the gift of a hairy face this Christmas.

NUTCRACKER JEWELLERS

Engraved gold bauble pendants, starting at just 5 peppermints. Choose from our most popular festive slogans, including: Ho, Ho, Ho, Jingle All the Way and I ♡ Santa.

AUTOMATIC TREE DECORATOR

Know someone tired of redecorating their tree every morning? Scared they'll forget and face the Krampuses' wrath? Then get them the automatic tree decorator!*

*Not yet approved by the Krampus Alliance. 70% bauble smash rate

This ingenious fake festive arm will do the heavy lifting for you!

Whenever they passed a sign with jaws clamping down on a cracker, they ducked.

After an hour or so, Gryla began getting used to the speed and pressure on her face.

'We haven't seen a single Krampus,' she said to Merrilee. 'That's lucky!'

And then everything went black.

Chapter 16

Krampus Sleigh Stop

'Krampus Sleigh Stop,' came an automated voice and the lights flicked back on.

Much to Gryla's horror they'd been manoeuvred into a garage filled with grainy screens monitoring the highways. And clattering around them was a Krampus! Each of its eyes was fixed on a different screen.

A pair of large doors stood open in front of them. In the distance Gryla could see the highway.

She shot Merrilee a look, but Merrilee shook her head.

'Too risky,' she whispered.

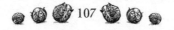

Gryla quickly slipped the Book under the sleigh's seat. 'Stay there,' she whispered to it. 'Don't you bounce back, our lives depend on it.'

'You have been stopped as part of a randomised sleigh stop,' came the automated voice. 'A Krampus will now inspect your sleigh and assess your festiveness.'

Merrilee looked worried. Gryla's candy-cane dress was very festive, but poor Merrilee was dressed in black and covered in soot! Without being able to play the Santa's daughter card, she was very clearly breaking the law. There was nothing festive about soot, and the Krampus Code pinned to the wall said as much.

KRAMPUS CODE

RULE TWO: FESTIVE ATTIRE

You must be obviously festive in your attire. Approved items include:
Festive jumpers with unique puns

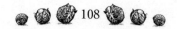

Red, green, gold and silver coloured garments

Shiny stuff

Festive pyjamas (although pyjamas are technically for bedtime, it's encouraged that these are worn at all times)

Shoes with bells on

Santa hats

Accessories such as white beards, black boots, hefty buckles

SOOT EXCEPTION: Introduced in 3004, the Soot Exception states that soot is NOT considered festive. A soot penalty may be applied to those who have no good reason to be covered in it. Please see rule 305 on how to best clean your chimney and rule 974 for products most effective for cleaning soot-covered clothing.

Quickly, Gryla grabbed Tinselcat and plonked him on Merrilee's head. Merrilee frantically brushed the soot from her smock and stood tall as the Krampus looked up.

Merrilee bowed, holding on to Tinselcat so he didn't fall off.

The Krampus moved closer, its fangs skimming Merrilee's shoulders as it sniffed.

It pulled out a control panel and tapped.

'Good festive hat,' came the automated voice, and Merrilee practically collapsed with relief.

It turned to Gryla, one eye on her, the rest still on the screens.

'Good festive dress,' the automated voice announced.

It pressed a button and a huge Christmas pudding swung down on a rope, knocking them both out of the sleigh.

'Occupants removed from sleigh,' the automated voice chimed, as Gryla and Merrilee landed with a crunch in the corner. They got to their feet and held their breath as the Krampus sniffed around the sleigh.

Merrilee tried to arrange Tinselcat on her head in a fashion that suited them both.

'I will put my tail up if I want to!' Tinselcat hissed.

The Krampus's eye shot to where the noise had come from.

Merrilee tilted her head innocently, her hat now much taller and pointier than it had been.

'Everything OK?' she squeaked.

The Krampus stared at the hat for a second, then – satisfied the sticky-up bit was fine – jumped into the sleigh, both feet landing at the same time with a terrifying thud.

Gryla winced.

'It mustn't find the Book,' she whispered to Merrilee.

Merrilee nodded in agreement and began to haul the Christmas pudding towards them.

The Krampus sniffed some more, and Gryla watched helplessly as he reached a claw under the seat and hooked the Book out from its hiding place. He gave it a

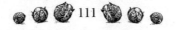

good sniff. Slowly, one by one, his eyes turned, until every single one was staring at it.

'CHARGE!' Merrilee shouted, swinging the Christmas pudding at the Krampus. It knocked the beast to the ground.

They scrambled for the sleigh. Gryla scooped up the Book and shoved it back under the seat.

The Krampus jumped to its feet and raced to the control panel. It punched a button and an alarm sounded.

Instantly, the garage doors slammed shut.

'There's no way out!' Gryla cried.

Merrilee grabbed the reins and guided the reindeer around the room at a speedy canter.

'What are you doing?' Gryla cried. 'We're going in circles!'

'Did you know that all buildings have to have a chimney?' she said.

'This one doesn't!' Gryla said.

'Exactly,' Merrilee said. 'Which means that it does. Probably just sealed up now. Reindeer are skilled at sniffing them out.'

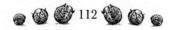

As she said it, the reindeer ground to a halt and began nudging the wall opposite the control panel.

The alarm blared.

'It's called its friends!' Gryla cried, watching the screens as thousands of Krampuses flew down the highway towards them. 'Look! They're coming!'

Merrilee positioned the sleigh so they had their backs to the wall.

'Three, two, one, back up!' she cried, pulling at the reins and sending the reindeer's bottoms crashing into the sleigh.

'You're going to break it!' Gryla cried as the whole thing went hurtling back into the wall. Pieces of the wall fell away.

'Again!' Merrilee called, and the reindeer ploughed backwards.

The Krampus was close now, its claws outstretched. One more step and it would be within grabbing distance.

Gryla squeezed her eyes shut.

'AGAIN!' Merrilee roared.

Gryla peeked, just in time to see the Krampus's claw hovering at her nose.

'AAAAAARGH!' she screamed, and a powerful force pulled her backwards.

WHOOSH!

Up they went, through soot and darkness and spider-webs galore, then –

Plop!

They slipped out on to the roof of the Krampus Sleigh Stop.

'I love chimneys,' Merrilee said with a smile.

She cracked the reins and they shot off to meet the highway again.

'That was close,' Gryla fretted. 'It won't be long until they find us – did you see how many were coming?'

'They'll split up,' Merrilee said. 'When they see we're not at the Krampus Sleigh Stop, they'll split up to look for us. At most we'll have to fight one or two. Maybe five.'

'FIGHT THEM?!' Gryla screeched.

'Yeah,' Merrilee said. 'Don't worry. I know all their routines, the shifts, the strategies. We can lose them again.'

They cruised along in silence. Gryla watched as her short, sharp breaths frosted in front of her.

After a little while, the traffic began to thin out as sleighs took the turn-offs to their destinations.

A couple of hours later, there was no one.

'Looks like we're the only ones going to the North Pole,' Merrilee said.

Gryla leaned back in her seat, Tinselcat cuddled on her lap. It was beautiful up there – watery skies, bright white snow … and total silence.

Too much silence.

'I have a weird feeling,' Gryla whispered.

'What?' Merrilee said.

Gryla looked around just as a hunched lump of wiry hair and claws hit the sleigh, sending it into a downward spiral.

'AAAAAAAARGH!' they screamed.

Merrilee quickly righted the sleigh and they looked up to see three Krampuses looming over them, their fangs dripping in sticky drool.

'KRAMPUS!' Merrilee shouted, snapping the reins and sending the reindeer shooting off again. Gryla clung on to the back of the sleigh, watching the Krampuses tearing through the sky behind them, grunting and wheezing.

'They're too fast and too close!' Tinselcat shouted. 'We won't be able to outfly them! They're made of magic!'

'He's right!' Merrilee shouted. 'What was I thinking?! Nothing can move as fast as a Krampus. They can fly ten times faster than anything else! Lightning speed! The Rudolphs can't outpace them!'

'What about a spell?!' Gryla said, hastily pulling the Book from under the seat. Her hands shook as she sifted through the recipes.

'Dangerous Sprout Soufflé, 'Twas the Night Before Cauldrons,' she mumbled, reading the spells. 'Frosty

Sprout …' Her shoulders sagged. Even if she found a useful spell, the lists of ingredients were all far too long!

'The Book is useless!' she cried, hurling it in frustration. In one clean sweep it knocked a Krampus from the sky and boomeranged back to her.

'That'll do,' Merrilee said.

Gryla leaned over the edge and watched the Krampus hit the fresh snow with a satisfying *puff*.

She took out the second with a *thwack*, sending it spiralling backwards, where it hit a highway sign with a *twang*.

But the third had seen what happened to its friends and ducked as the Book came hurtling towards it.

It bounced back to Gryla.

She tried again. The Krampus dodged.

'Quickly, Gryla!' Merrilee said.

'I can't look!' Tinselcat cried, ducking under the seat.

The Krampus bounded back, snapping and snarling.

'It keeps moving!' Gryla said, failing to hit it again.

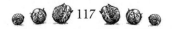

'Ugh!' Merrilee said. 'Krampuses are so annoying!' She pulled the sleigh to an abrupt halt.

Gryla recoiled as the Krampus kept coming at speed. Its hairy legs tried to back-pedal, but it was no good. It bounced off the sleigh with a satisfying *boing*.

Gryla launched the Book again, and this time she hit it. The Krampus spun round and round, a hairy blur of matted fur, before landing with a thud next to its friend.

'Hardbacks are handy,' Gryla said, as the reindeer lengthened their stride and headed North.

Chapter 17

I Spy with My Krampus Eyes

'Are we there yet?' Tinselcat groaned. He lifted a paw and admired his fierce tinselclaws.

'We're one minute closer than when you asked last time,' Gryla said.

'I've been thinking about the Krampuses,' Tinselcat said. 'It's not their fault they were created as monsters, so maybe it's not right to destroy them.'

Merrilee frowned. 'But the Krampuses were

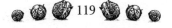

created with magic. They're no more real than a holographic elf.'

'Or a Tinselcat,' Tinselcat said quietly.

'MERRILEE!' came a shout, and with a *pop*, Fred the elf materialised at her feet. He was glitching and almost invisible.

'You … seem … to … be out of … range-*ssssssswaaaaash* … Toy?'

'Oh, no thank you, Fred.'

Even though he was glitching his disappointed face was clear.

'Later,' Merrilee said. 'I promise.'

'Fine,' Fred said in an exasperated tone and he disappeared with a *pop*.

'Let's play a game,' Gryla said, trying to lighten the mood. 'Anyone have any good sleigh games?'

'I Spy with My Krampus Eyes?' Merrilee cheered.

'What are the rules?' Tinselcat asked.

'You say "I spy with my Krampus eyes" and then you list fifty things.'

'Fifty?!' Gryla cried. Their version of I Spy with My Witchy Eyes was only one thing.

'Yes, fifty because Krampuses have a lot of eyes,' Merrilee said.

Tinselcat stood tall. 'I'll start. I spy with my Krampus eyes something beginning with S and G and M and S again and H and—'

'This is going to be a long journey,' Gryla groaned.

Chapter 18

A Jolly Announcement

They were nearly twelve hours into the journey when Gryla started to feel sleigh-sick.

Round they went.

And down.

And up.

And through a cloud.

And over a hump.

And down again.

For hours and hours and hours.

'I'm going to be sick!' Gryla yelled.

'We'll stop over there!' Merrilee said, pointing up ahead.

Gryla looked up, her face as green as a witch stereotype.

Flashing in lights of red and gold were the greatest words she'd ever seen.

SANTA STOP HERE

'We're halfway!' Merrilee cheered. 'After this stop there's only another twelve hours to go!'

Gryla tried to smile, but vomited instead.

'BLEEEEURGH!'

Merrilee guided the reindeer down to a small igloo suspended in the sky on a candy-cane pole. In the icy depths below, Gryla couldn't see where it was secured.

There was nothing around them, just night sky and the distant flicker of lights that marked out the highway beyond.

There was just one other sleigh parked outside. It wasn't as colourful or as grand as theirs. It was bright green with a sloppily painted red trim and covered in glitter. Gryla thought it must belong to whoever worked there. It had holographic reindeer tied to it, who munched on holographic carrots dispensed from a little machine.

As soon as her boots hit solid ground, Gryla felt better.

'Just a quick stop,' Merrilee said to the Rudolphs.

'Can they eat those?' Gryla asked as a holographic carrot rolled out and lay flashing at their hoofs.

Both reindeer looked at her like she was silly.

'No, they're real, so they just eat real things. I'll see if they have any carrot-flavoured candy canes inside,' Merrilee said, giving them each a pat.

They slid along the icy path to a door, frosted and heavy. It jingled when Gryla pushed it open.

The place was like an igloo inside too, all domed ice and low ceilings. It reminded her of the caves at home. There was a simple icy counter with a small Christmas tree decorated with shabby ornaments. Two ice tables with chairs sat in the middle of the room and behind the counter hundreds of candy canes hung from hooks – striped in every shade of brown.

'Mince-pie and chocolate flavour canes, that's all we've got here,' came a voice, and Gryla turned to see a waitress standing behind her. She was tall and wore a Santa beard. 'Welcome to the Santa Stop. Don't get many round these parts. Have you come far?'

'Uh, sort of … from Humbug,' Merrilee muttered, not keen to get into specifics.

'Nice! Christmas capital of the world, no better place to be,' the waitress said. 'Take a seat and I'll get you a hot drink – melted hot chocolate-flavoured candy canes all right with you?'

'YES!' Gryla and Merrilee said at once.

'You sound hungry,' the waitress said. 'Must've been a long ride.'

'Tell me about it,' Gryla said, forcing a smile.

They took a seat and the waitress hurried off to get their drinks.

Gryla stared out of the window. The skies were clear of blizzards there – jet black and filled with stars. She could even see the moon.

'Wait,' she said. 'What's that on the moon?'

Merrilee groaned. 'Oh, it's new,' she said. 'Dad wanted to make it more festive.'

'Is it a Santa hat?' Gryla said, trying not to laugh.

Merrilee's cheeks went red. 'It was a passion project of his. He'd put hats on the stars if their heat wouldn't incinerate them.'

Gryla puffed out her cheeks to stop herself from laughing.

'You're laughing!' Merrilee said, jabbing her arm. 'It's not funny, it's weird! Honestly, Dad used to be normal. But being Santa messes with your head.'

'*How* did they get it into space?' Gryla asked.

'Didn't you see the TV show?' the waitress said, plonking the drinks down. 'It was called *Eight Gingerbread Rockets and a Giant Santa Hat Go to Space*. A whole hour-long documentary. *Very* interesting …' She sauntered off.

'See,' Gryla said. 'A fan of the Santa hat on the moon, and associated broadcasting.'

Merrilee laughed and slurped her drink. 'This is nice,' she said with a smile. 'I don't get to chat with friends much. I mean, I don't really have friends.'

'Really?' Gryla said, sitting up in surprise. 'But you're Santa's daughter, everyone must be desperate to be your friend.'

Merrilee laughed. 'Exactly. Everyone just wants to know me because I'm Santa's daughter, not because they really know or like me at all. But what about you?' Merrilee asked. 'I bet you have lots of witchy friends on the Mince Pie Isles?'

'Not a single one,' Gryla said. 'All the witches my age think I'm weird.'

'Even now you're the *chosen* witch with that *special* spell book?'

Now it was Gryla's turn to laugh. 'No, they're just terrified by the whole thing, last I heard.'

'JINGLE JINGLE!' came a roar and the old TV hanging above the counter burst into life.

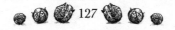

'The best time of the day!' the waitress cheered. 'Look, it's him – my darling Santa!'

There, filling the whole screen with rosy cheeks and a pillowy white beard was none other than Santa Claus himself.

'Dad,' Merrilee whispered in surprise.

'Ho ho ho, Merry Christmas!' he boomed. 'It's me, Santa Claus, with my daily festive address to the nation.'

'He's OK,' Gryla said with relief. But Merrilee looked suspicious.

'He doesn't look OK,' she said. 'He's reading it off a script, watch his eyes! I bet Klaus is making him do this.'

'I do hope you've all had a lovely festive day, full of your favourite candy canes. And I do hope you haven't been naughty and upset the Krampus Alliance.'

'Never!' the waitress said. 'I'm basically trapped in the middle of nowhere in an igloo, so I can't really commit crimes anyway!'

'Today's announcement is that SuperElf branded holographic elves are being recalled. They have developed a glitch that makes them enact revenge on anyone who asks them for anything … Ho ho ho. So don't use those ones.'

Gryla watched as Santa cleared his throat awkwardly and read on.

'I would also like to announce that as of today I will be stepping down as Santa Claus—'

'KNEW IT!' Merrilee cried, pointing madly at the screen. 'Klaus! He's just hauled him up from the dungeons to do this and then he'll haul him back down. Or worse!'

'Klaus, my most senior palace Snowman, will be your Santa from now on. There is no greater person to fill the role, no one more handsome, or funny or wise, or brilliant.'

Gryla gagged.

'He will be the greatest Santa Claus the world has ever seen.' Santa took a big gulp of air. 'And he has my full support.'

'Why doesn't he say something?' Merrilee fretted. 'Why doesn't he tell us what's really happening?'

'And finally,' Santa said, 'before I go, I have a serious and very personal request. My daughter has vanished, kidnapped from the palace by a witch. The Krampuses have assured me that even though I will no longer be Santa, they will help me find her and bring her home safely.'

'So that's how Klaus got him to lie!' Merrilee said. 'He's promised he'll get me home safely. That's the oldest trick in the book, Dad!'

'If you have any information, please contact the palace, or alert a nearby Krampus,' Santa said.

Pictures of Merrilee, Gryla and their sleigh flashed up on-screen.

Gryla glanced nervously to the waitress, whose eyes were wide, looking from Gryla to Merrilee to the sleigh outside and back again.

'Time to go,' Merrilee whispered, and they bolted for the door.

'THANK YOU!' Gryla shouted. 'AND MERRY CHRISTMAS!'

The waitress looked dazed. 'I didn't know witches had manners!'

Chapter 19

Back on the Mince Pie Isles

Back on the Mince Pie Isles, the witches were searching for Gryla.

'I still can't believe she got the Book,' Cackle said, ducking down under the candy-cane vines to look for her.

Up and down the neat rows of vines were equally neat lines of witches, searching around every stalk.

Gryla's grandmother was up at the front.

'I don't see how she could've been hiding for so long, it's so unlike her to go missing.'

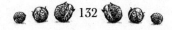

'The Book can change a witch,' one of the elder witches mused as she snapped off a candy cane and took a nibble. 'She'll come back when she's ready.'

'What if someone else finds her first?' Cackle fretted. 'And the Book. Think what the world could do to us!'

'The Book chose Gryla for a reason,' the elder witch said. 'The ghost of Befana is wise.'

Cackle snorted.

'OVER HERE!' a witch cried, and the coven came running.

The witch had carefully scraped away a top layer of snow, revealing a pair of boots.

'Those are Gryla's boots!' her grandmother cried.

The witches crowded around.

'Maybe the blizzard lifted her off somewhere?'

'No …' Cackle said slowly. 'A blizzard would blow you sideways first. These are upright. It looks like … she went straight up.'

They all looked up to the sky.

'How is that possible?' her grandmother said.

'I hope it wasn't anything to do with the strange girl we saw in the bauble …' the pink-haired bauble witch whispered to the other.

'Just thinking about the security risks,' said the red-haired one. 'Shouldn't someone be manning the candy-cane cannon defences rather than the whole coven looking for Gryla?'

Gryla's grandmother's eyes grew wide. 'LISTEN!' she said, raising a hand to silence everyone.

The coven fell silent, their eyes still skyward.

Amid the whistle of the winds and sharp tings of clinking candy canes came another noise. Something distant but growing louder.

A low, heavy grunting noise.

'I've never heard anything like it,' an elder witch whispered, just as something sliced through the sky.

They saw the glint of a claw.

'KRAMPUS!' Cackle screamed, as a mass of eyes and fangs came crashing down on them.

Chapter 20

Eggnogs

The North Pole stretched out beneath Gryla, its snowy peaks scattered across the land like a badly iced cake.

The three occupants of the sleigh leaned over the edge, hoping they might see something.

Gryla could sense there was meant to be more.

'I'm not sure why we're looking from this height,' Tinselcat said. 'Would we spot a tiny elf from up here?'

Gryla scanned the terrain carefully for hints of life. It

was vast and empty. Although she'd planned for them to come here, now they'd arrived she suddenly felt lost. But she didn't want to say so, as she didn't want to let Merrilee down.

'All right, elf expert,' Merrilee said, rubbing her hands together excitedly. 'Show me the elves!'

Gryla kept looking. 'Uh, still trying to find them.'

'Really?' Merrilee said. 'Do they usually hide?'

'Um, I'm not exactly—'

'She doesn't know,' Tinselcat said. 'I think she's hoping something will jump out at her.'

'ARGH!' Gryla screamed, making the others leap in fright.

'What?' Merrilee asked, racing to Gryla's side of the sleigh.

'Christmas trees!' Gryla pointed frantically.

In the distance stood a strange clump of ancient-looking fir trees with tips that seemed to skim the stars. They were covered in decorations – baubles and ornaments, hundreds of them.

'I wonder who decorated them?' Gryla said, her eyes narrowing. Merrilee steered the sleigh down to take a better look.

It skidded through the thick snow like a trusty plough and was brought to a halt as it gently bumped into a tree. An ornament – a simple little angel – dropped from a branch and smashed at their feet, making them all jump.

Slowly, they looked up.

'It's the biggest Christmas tree I've ever seen,' Gryla whispered in awe.

The sleigh shook. Gryla grabbed the side.

'Did you feel that?' she said.

The Rudolphs snorted in alarm.

Then, quite extraordinarily, the tree sidestepped! And kept sidestepping, further and further away from the sleigh.

Gryla and Merrilee looked at each other.

Then another tree started moving. And another!

And within a few seconds, all the Christmas trees were galloping into the distance!

'But … how?' Merrilee said.

'Magic!' Gryla cried. She leaped from the sleigh and ran after them. 'Come back! We don't want to hurt you!'

The trees were big, but Gryla was faster. Soon she'd caught up and was pinballing between their trunks.

'Please! I need your help!' she begged.

At that, some of the trees stopped.

Merrilee arrived out of breath. 'I didn't know trees could move so fast.'

'We can be speedy,' came a voice, and Gryla looked up to see the tree had eyes, crowned with long, bushy eyelashes.

'ARGH!' she screamed again.

'You're not trees!' Merrilee cried.

'We're Eggnogs,' said a smaller tree, his pine-needle lips lolloping up and down as he spoke. 'And we're definitely trees. Christmas trees, in fact. I'm Small Eggnog. She's Big Eggnog, that's Flat Eggnog – he likes lying down. Over there is Bouncy Eggnog, and Twirly Eggnog and Best Eggnog, he named himself. You've got Bald Eggnog …'

Gryla noticed one that had no needles at all, but was nevertheless covered in decorations.

'We're all called *Something* Eggnog, apart from Eggnog the First, because he was the first Eggnog. He just goes by Eggnog.'

The trees parted and a huge fir tree stepped forward. His eyes were old, twig-lined with thinning needles.

'WHY ARE YOU CHASING MY FAMILY?' his voice boomed.

Gryla and Merrilee took a step back.

'I'm Gryla, and this is my friend Merrilee,' Gryla said, her voice shaking. 'We need to find the elves, it's urgent.'

'The elves made us!' Twiggy Eggnog said.

'A LONG TIME AGO,' Eggnog said sadly. Gryla's heart sank. Maybe they were really gone after all.

'CAROL WAS HER NAME. SHE WAS MY MUMMY,' Eggnog said.

'What happened to her?' Gryla asked softly.

Tears welled in Eggnog's old eyes. 'THEY TOOK HER CENTURIES AGO. SHE WENT TO A PLACE

CALLED HUMBUG AND THEY SQUEEZED THE MAGIC OUT OF HER, AND USED IT TO MAKE MONSTERS. SHE ESCAPED, BUT WHEN SHE GOT HOME SHE WAS WEAK. BEFORE SHE DIED, SHE USED THE LAST DROP OF MAGIC IN HER TO MAKE ME A PRESENT. MY TINSELCAT! BUT A STORM TOOK HIM AWAY LONG AGO.'

'Could you stop running so fast, Gryla? My tinsel legs can only take so—' Tinselcat stopped dead.

Eggnog shrieked.

Tinselcat's tinsel hair stood on end.

'HE'S BACK,' Eggnog said. He reached down a branch and scooped Tinselcat into a hug.

'It's the tree!' Tinselcat said. 'I remember this tree!'

'You mean, Tinselcat was made by an elf?' Gryla said.

Eggnog sobbed. 'YES! I HAVEN'T SEEN HIM FOR YEARS!'

Tinselcat began climbing through Eggnog's branches. 'I remember it! I remember this branch, and this one and this one!'

He leaped out and landed at Gryla's feet. She scooped him up. She'd never considered Tinselcat might belong to someone else, and she certainly didn't want to part with him.

'WHERE DID YOU GO?' Eggnog asked.

'The Mince Pie Isles, with the witches!' Tinselcat said.

Gryla winced. The last thing she needed was the trees knowing she was a witch, but much to her surprise, Eggnog chuckled.

'THAT EXPLAINS WHY YOU CAN TALK NOW.' He turned to Gryla. 'HOT CHOCOLATE?'

Gryla and Merrilee stood back and watched as the trees busied themselves laying out mugs and marshmallows, chocolate sprinkles and whipped cream.

'Real food,' Merrilee said in amazement. 'I've never seen food that isn't shaped like a candy cane!'

'Where do you get your decorations from?' Gryla asked as she plucked a marshmallow from a small plate. 'And where do you get all this real food from?'

'UM,' Eggnog said. 'SHOPS?'

'Oh my stockings!' Merrilee said, biting into a marsh-mallow. 'It's so fluffy! Look how stretchy it is! It's unbelievable!' She began laughing hysterically. 'Oooh, and it's gooey!'

'TRY PUTTING SOME IN YOUR HOT CHOCOLATE,' Eggnog said with a knowing smile.

Merrilee tried it and almost melted into the snow.

'Thank you for making us feel so welcome,' Gryla said. 'This is the kind of magical place I thought the rest of the Christmas world would be, but it wasn't.'

'WITCHES ARE ALWAYS WELCOME HERE,' Eggnog said with a smile, nudging a mug towards her. 'WITCHES ARE WONDERFUL.'

Gryla could feel the cold, horrible feeling she felt every time she heard the word 'witch' melting away. She'd never heard witches being talked about so favour-ably by anyone other than witches.

'MORE?' Eggnog said as Gryla finished her hot chocolate in one gulp.

She realised something … the mugs were minuscule. And the shaker of sprinkles was small too, and the marshmallows …

'Hey!' Gryla said. 'How do such big trees make such small things?'

'BUSTED!' came a tiny voice from somewhere in the trees. 'SEE? I *TOLD* YOU, MAKE THEM BIGGER THAN YOUR HEAD OR ELSE THEY'LL BE SUSPICIOUS.'

Gryla turned to Merrilee and beamed.

'I knew it,' she whispered. 'I knew it!'

Chapter 21

Carol, Carol, Carol, Carol

Gryla stared up at the trees. The more she looked, the more she could see movement. Leaves quivering, a tiny tuft of red striped hair sticking out like a small bird. A dangling leg.

Eggnog coughed loudly.

'Are they in there?' Gryla mouthed.

He bowed his head in shame – and an elf fell out.

'EGGNOG!' the elf cried from where she had splatted in the hot chocolate. She climbed out and shook herself off.

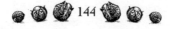

'SORRY,' Eggnog said. 'BUT DON'T WORRY, THEY ARE WITCHES!'

'Err,' Merrilee began, but Gryla nudged her.

'And not just any witches!' an elf cried, pointing at the Book. 'That's *the* witch.'

A chorus of whispers started up and quickly grew to a deafening chatter.

'You know about the Book?' Gryla said in surprise.

'Oh yes,' the elf said. 'That's a very famous book – the Brussels Sprout Brew helped defeat the evil Mr Krampus a long time ago. Back when we made toys.'

Everyone fell silent.

'Such a long time ago,' the elf said sadly. 'Then the Krampus Alliance was created. They used Carol to make them – and she died because of it. We've been in hiding ever since so they don't do the same to us!'

Gryla and Merrilee stood back as all around them tiny elves poked their heads out from every tree to get a better look at them.

'Am I glad to see you,' Gryla said.

Merrilee stuck her head into one of the trees.

'There's a whole village in here!' she cried.

Gryla took a look. Merrilee was right. There were little wooden houses, some had sap hot tubs. Reams and reams of twinkly technicolour lights were strung up along the branches. There were steps carved into branches and lifts in the trunks.

'We used to live in a secret and snowy village,' an elf said right in Gryla's ear, making her jump. 'But this is safer. No one expects to find an elf living in a tree.'

'I miss our old home,' another said sadly. 'No offence, Eggnogs, but you do spin a lot.'

'We only ever go back for Snowcus Pocus,' a third added.

'What's that?' Gryla asked.

'It's how we get our elf magic for the year. Every year on Christmas Day, elves build snowmen and burrow inside them. For that one special day, our magic charges up and we have enough to last a year.'

'But now that we don't have to fly a sleigh around the

world or make toys, we have more magic than we know what to do with,' an elf sighed. 'I just use mine for making hot chocolate now.'

'The wrong size hot chocolate,' a nearby elf said pointedly.

'We used to have a huge workshop,' another elf said. They began chattering excitedly as the memories came back to them.

'A huge dining table where we had feasts!'

'And a big ice chimney obstacle course where our favourite Claus would practise the present-delivery system.'

'Can we see it?' Merrilee asked. 'It sounds incredible!'

The elves exchanged glances.

'No one has visited in hundreds of years. We have two elves on the inside, who guard what's left of the place, in case one day we might return. I'm not sure they'd like us bringing people in.'

'Let's make it a game!' another elf cried. 'If they can pass the guard elves' defences then they're allowed in.'

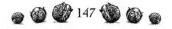

'Isn't that just the security system that already exists?' another elf muttered.

'Down there,' an elf said, pointing at Gryla's boots.

'Here?' Gryla reached down and dug into the snow. A small candy cane striped in red and white rose up until it was level with her head. Gryla tried to lift it but it was stuck in the ground.

Suddenly, the thing began to swivel like a periscope and she had to duck to avoid its hook.

'What is it?' Gryla asked.

'HELLO,' boomed a very small voice from the candy cane. 'I AM THE GIANT CANDY CANE OF DOOM. LEAVE OUR LANDS, PLEASE AND THANK YOU.'

'Don't say please and thank you!' hissed another voice through the candy cane.

'I SAID PLEASE AND THANK YOU BECAUSE I AM POLITE, BUT I AM ALSO A VERY SCARY CANDY CANE OF DOOM.'

'Candy cane of doom?' Gryla said with a smile.

'THAT'S RIGHT, I AM THE CANDY—'

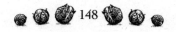

'You should've said haunted candy cane,' came the other voice. 'It's too vague to just be a candy cane of doom. She doesn't even sound scared. I would've said "Candy Cane Assistant to the *Monster* of Doom".'

Suddenly, the candy cane clicked. The ground began to quake. Gryla grabbed Merrilee's hand. Decorations and elves began to drop from the trees. Gryla bent her knees to steady herself, but it was no good, the snow beneath her feet whipped her up into the air. She caught flashes of Tinselcat and Merrilee as the whole world spun into a blur of trees and snow flurries. She hit the ground and looked up to see a darkened town and a frosty fortress of ice chimneys.

'Welcome to Carolburg,' an elf said.

The elves swarmed around them.

'Before we show you round, please will you tell us your names?' an elf asked them.

'I'm Merrilee,' Merrilee said confidently, her eyes fixed on the cool ice chimneys. 'And this is Gryla.'

'I'm so sorry,' Gryla said, recognising a few of the elves she had spoken to earlier. 'We haven't even asked *your* names yet.'

At that, the entire clump of elves erupted into hysterical laughter.

'Is something … funny?' Gryla muttered.

'We're all called Carol,' an elf said.

'All of you?' Gryla said. 'There's hundreds of you.'

'Yes,' Carol said. 'We're the Carols. Very easy.'

'We just love the name!' an elf shouted from the back.

'Is that the ice chimney obstacle course?' Merrilee asked excitedly.

The Carols nodded.

It was a long line of ice chimneys, each one more complicated than the last.

'It was used to perfect the delivery of presents, when the world knew only of a Santa in the North Pole. We built it to make sure all the chimneys in the world could be visited in one night.'

'Cool!' Merrilee said. 'May I?'

The Carols shrugged.

'I don't see why not,' one said. 'But it's very slippy and treacherous – watch the chimneys with the tight bends, take it slowl—'

But Merrilee had already charged off. The elves watched in awe as she shot up and dived down and squeezed through each chimney with ease.

'Is it meant to be … difficult?' Gryla whispered.

But the Carols were speechless.

They raced to meet Merrilee as she popped out at the far end.

Merrilee was bent over, resting her hands on her knees. 'That was pretty tough,' she panted. 'How did I do?'

The Carols just stared, mouths ajar.

'I presume you've got a best time recorded,' Merrilee said. 'Did I beat it?'

'I've never seen anything like it,' a Carol squeaked in awe.

They all moved closer.

'It'll be because she's a witch,' one said. 'We've never had a witch try it.'

'I'm not a witch,' Merrilee said, without thinking.

A frostiness fell upon the group.

Gryla watched the Carols' expressions change from amazed to horrified. Quickly, they backed away.

'What?' Merrilee said. 'Have I done something?'

'SHE'S NOT A WITCH! SHE'S A CHRISTMAS WORLD ONE!'

The Carols flew into a panic, whipping up snow like smoke clouds as they raced to hide.

'YOU SAW NOTHING!' came a cry. 'THE ELVES ARE DEAD!'

'Ooops,' Merrilee said.

'I think they'll come around,' said a voice, and Gryla turned to see an old elf at her feet. 'I'm Carol – I like to invent things and I'm very wise. I invented tinsel paper – secret writing paper that shreds on reading. It's what Carol made your cat out of.'

'I wondered why I could see writing on him!' Gryla said.

'Would you like a tour of the town?' he said, giving Merrilee a smile. 'Any friend of a witch in this world is a friend of ours.'

'I'd love to do the ice chimneys again,' Merrilee said as she bounced from foot to foot. Gryla had never seen her so happy.

'Be my guest,' Inventor Carol said. 'Now, Gryla, would you like a tour of the town? I have an idea to get the other Carols to come out again.'

'FREE RIDE ON TINSELCAT!'

Nothing.

'JUMP ABOARD THE TINSELCAT!'

'I remember taking the Carols for rides!' Tinselcat cheered. 'So much is coming back to me.'

But no one was taking the bait.

'Usually, they wouldn't be able to resist,' Inventor Carol said.

Suddenly, an elf burst from a gingerbread house and dived on to Tinselcat's back.

'TRAITOR!' came a cry.

The Carol shrugged. 'It's too fun to resist.'

'So, over here we have the ice rink,' Inventor Carol said, continuing with the tour.

The town square, even in its neglected state, was the most magical place Gryla had ever seen. Next to the ice rink, surrounded by technicolour icicles strung up like bunting, was a long dining table. It was piled high with snow and unusable.

The remnants of snowmen from the Snowcus Pocus ceremony were visible in the distance, in neat little rows.

A few more Carols ran to Tinselcat and jumped on his back. Then a few more.

Inventor Carol winked at Gryla.

'Now this here is where we once made toys for all the children in the world,' he boasted. 'I even made toys for the ones on the naughty list, depending on the crimes.'

The toy workshop was half buried in snow, and the *T* in *Toy* was faded on the old sign.

'Come and see,' the elf said, throwing himself at the door. It swung open with an uncomfortable crunch.

More Carols clustered on to Tinselcat, some peeking around the door to take a look at the old workshop.

It was a sad sight. The workbenches sat empty, and half-made toys were scattered on the floor. But the saddest part of all was the stack of unanswered letters, from children long gone.

'They asked for a special toy to be delivered to their stocking by night. But what they got that year was a whole new world order and a holographic elf that churned out toys whenever they wanted.'

Gryla picked up a carefully decorated letter. Hours of colouring work and list-making had gone into sending this to the magical North Pole. It was a small piece of paper filled with hope and belief in magic. Then she remembered the reality of the Christmas world she had seen. She remembered what she'd said to her grandmother, about her being too old to understand, when really her grandmother had been right all along.

'Why are you here?' Carol asked.

'We want to destroy the Krampuses,' Merrilee said, panting in the doorway. 'By the way, I think I just beat my previous time.'

'Unbelievable!' a Carol said.

Merrilee walked into the workshop, making the elves jump out of the way. 'If we could defeat the Krampuses,' she said, 'we could bring back the magic of Christmas once a year, with a real Santa and toys in stockings again, then this workshop could be brought back to life. You could be Christmas elves again!'

The Carols began to chatter excitedly.

'You know,' one said seriously, 'I always said something was wrong when they started putting Christmas things in shops at Halloween ...'

'But because the Krampuses were made with elf magic, we need elf magic to destroy them,' Gryla explained. 'We need you.'

The Carols exchanged excited glances.

'Are you in?' Gryla said.

'YES!' they cried.

Gryla and Merrilee hugged and spun around the room.

'But where do we begin?' Gryla said.

'I don't know,' said Inventor Carol. 'But I really feel we should call it OPERATION BRING DOWN SANTA CLAUS … if everyone else agrees?'

'YES!' the Carols roared.

Chapter 22

Operation Bring Down Santa Claus

Merrilee laid out a large piece of tinsel paper on a workshop bench and began to draw.

'This is everything I know about the Krampuses.'

Everyone huddled round.

'They live in a lair on the south side of the river in Humbug. The lair is marked by a series of black chimneys. It doesn't look much from above, but below ground it spreads like a fast fungus – the whole place is huge, over a mile long and dark, and growing. It's where the

Krampuses take the things they have confiscated and hide them forever. No one has ever been inside the lair, not even a Santa.'

'It's the perfect place to pounce on them!' Inventor Carol said. 'A confined space to use our magic would mean we could optimise its power. For it to work, we have to take all the Krampuses out at once.'

'They work in shifts,' Merrilee said. 'One shift returns and clocks back in to the lair, then the others wake up and leave. The switchover happens in no more than five seconds. They need twelve hours sleep to be fully functional.'

Gryla shot Inventor Carol a worried look.

'That could be a problem,' she said.

'It's impossible,' Inventor Carol said. 'There are too many variables, and we'd only have one shot. Five seconds is not enough time to make sure we can do it properly.'

Gryla slumped back in her chair, the disappointment soaking into her like melting snow.

But then her eyes grew wide. 'What if the Krampuses due to wake up and leave for their shift stayed asleep and never left the lair at shift change? Then the ones returning from their shift would all file into the lair. They'd all be there. The Carols could be lying in wait with the sleeping Krampuses and *BOOM*!'

'But how would you keep the sleeping ones asleep so they don't immediately wake up and leave the lair when the others come back?' Merrilee said.

'Yes,' a Carol said. 'That would require some sort of sleep magic, and we need every drop of our magic to get there and undo the Krampuses.'

'The Brussels Sprout Brew!' Gryla cried. She slammed her book down on the table and frantically began flicking through the pages.

'Yes!' Inventor Carol cried. 'That's the one that was used on Mr Krampus and saved Christmas thousands of years ago. It was powerful, it would be perfect – and poetic!'

Gryla flicked through the Book, the old, crisp pages flaking in her hands.

She stopped.

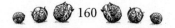

'You've found it?' Inventor Carol asked eagerly.

Gryla stared down at the page. She couldn't believe it. She hadn't noticed it before, but then again, she hadn't properly looked through the Book.

'It's ...' she began, unable to believe her eyes, 'half ripped out.'

'Oh no!' Inventor Carol cried.

Gryla held up the Book. There it was, a half-torn, jagged page. 'Half the recipe is missing!'

Inventor Carol slumped. 'That complicates things a bit.'

'Does anyone know the full recipe?' Gryla asked hopefully, but she was met with silence.

'Why would someone rip it?' Gryla said.

'Maybe it was an accident,' a Carol suggested.

Gryla shook her head. 'No, a witch would repair it in that case.'

'Maybe someone didn't want the spell to be used,' Merrilee said.

'But that makes no sense,' Gryla argued. 'Even if an

enemy found it, there would be no benefit to ripping out half a page – they'd have destroyed the whole Book.'

Inventor Carol frowned. 'That is strange. You'll need to look for it.'

He raced off and returned with a map.

'I say we start the search here,' he said, unfolding the map in front of them. 'The Brussels Sprout Brew was famously brewed here – in this house on Stratton Street.'

'It's called Sugarplum Street now,' Merrilee corrected him.

'The witch hid in the basement, pretending to be the house cook!' Gryla cried, remembering her grand-mother's tale.

'Bingo,' Inventor Carol said. 'We start there.'

Merrilee inspected the map. 'The house the witch lived in is the Christmas Lunch Club now – it was originally in the building next door, but the Santa before Dad loved it so much he expanded the restaurant to take up the whole street.'

'So the Christmas Lunch Club is your way in – just pretend you're having a nice meal,' Inventor Carol said.

'We won't be able to get close,' Gryla said, the fear rising in her when she thought about going near Humbug again.

'The Krampuses are looking for us,' Merrilee told them.

'Hmm,' Inventor Carol said, tapping his chin. 'I'll have to use my magic to whip you up a very special disguise …'

Chapter 23

The Christmas Lunch Club

The following day...

'I thought they were going to use their magic to give us completely different identities,' Merrilee said from the peephole in her giant turkey costume. 'This is fancy dress. Who uses the most powerful magic in the world to make a *fancy dress costume you can buy in a shop*?'

'Agreed. It's not what I would've chosen,' Gryla said from inside her matching outfit. 'At least we can't get in trouble with the Krampuses for not being festive.'

They parked the sleigh and reindeer under a nearby

bridge and walked through the snow to what was once Stratton Street.

The whole row of houses was ablaze with festive lights and a sign hanging on one of the doors read: *The Christmas Lunch Club*. Beyond the fairy-light-framed windows, diners were dressed in their finest Christmas outfits – a sea of silver and gold and red and green.

'It's seen as an institution because Mr Krampus once lived on this very street,' Merrilee whispered. 'The entrance to the place is supposed to have been the old door to his house.'

'And the one next door is where the Book was hidden!' Gryla said. 'You know, I think I'd feel more like we were saving Christmas if we weren't in giant turkey costumes,' she added.

'I like them,' Merrilee said. 'Who's going to suspect two girls dressed as turkeys are about to change the world?'

A waiter showed them to their table.

'And you said your surname was—?'

'Turkeytrois,' Merrilee said, making Gryla snort.

'Very unusual,' he said.

'It's from the glorious country of Noelle,' Merrilee lied. 'We're just visiting.'

'Oh, I hear the skiing in Noelle is fantastic. I'll go and get the specials menu.'

Gryla felt a strange sense of familiarity about the Christmas Lunch Club. It was as if the witchyness left behind long ago – the kindness, the secret brews, the *magic* – was in the bones of the place.

People were seated at long tables that stretched the length of the street; the dividing walls between each townhouse had been knocked down to create one mega-restaurant. The tables were piled high with platters of candy canes. Clatters and shouts rang out from the back as waiters and waitresses wearing Santa hats ran to and fro fetching orders for their hungry customers.

The crunching was as deafening as the music: traditional Christmas songs sung by Santa himself. Only now, the Santa singing them was Klaus.

'That's a weird relief,' Merrilee said.

The TV in the corner flickered to life and Klaus's face filled the screen.

'HO HO HO, MERRY CHRISTMAS!'

Merrilee growled.

'It is me, Santa, here to wish you a very Merry Christmas and to remind you all to be jolly, but also to be very alert and look for this witch.'

Gryla's face appeared on the screen, an unflattering close-up from a security camera outside the palace. She ducked, forgetting for a second that she was disguised as a giant turkey.

'I would also like to invite you all to the palace tomorrow afternoon for a *very special* ceremony to mark the start of my long reign as your beloved and all-powerful Santa Claus. Merry Christmas to you all.'

'We have to find a way to get to the basement,' Gryla whispered. 'That's where Uma Garland lived, and I bet that's where she made the brew. If the missing page is anywhere, it's down there.'

'I have an idea,' Merrilee said, swiping some candy-cane leftovers from a nearby table. Then she grabbed Gryla's arm and they barged through to the back.

A waiter was coming through a door with a huge tray of candy canes.

'Turkey-flavour candy-cane delivery,' Merrilee said.

The waiter raised an eyebrow. 'Down there, kitchens are on the left.'

They raced down in silence. Gryla could feel Merrilee's hand shaking in hers. They passed the kitchen, where candy canes bubbled in big vats and the chefs shouted out orders. Further down the corridor was a door marked: *CANDY-CANE CUPBOARD*.

It was a newish door, bright red and shiny.

'They must've added this to connect the houses. The basement of Uma's old house is here,' Gryla said, pushing the door open.

It creaked loudly. Inside, all was dark.

Merrilee rummaged around for a light switch. 'Aha,' she said, and light flooded the room.

Hanging on the walls and piled high in boxes littering the floor were millions and millions of candy canes.

They squeezed through, their turkey costumes snagging on every box they passed.

'I was expecting an empty, neglected room,' Gryla said. 'How are we going to find it?'

'Quickly,' Merrilee said, tipping out boxes of candy canes and knocking them off the walls. 'We mustn't get caught.'

Gryla joined in, upturning boxes and running her hands over every surface.

'If a small scrap of paper was hidden here, it's long gone!' she cried, and she kicked the wall. The whole lot of candy canes hanging there fell and smashed at her feet.

But behind the candy canes, there wasn't a bare wall. There was a watercolour painting of a Christmas feast. Gryla felt a tingle dance up her spine as she studied the painting.

'That's weird, it's stuck to the wall,' she said through gritted teeth, as she tried to move the frame. She felt a little indent and pushed.

With a creak, it swung open, revealing a secret compartment.

'Woah,' Merrilee said, racing over to inspect it.

They peered inside.

'This was where she hid the Book,' Gryla whispered. 'Look, it fits perfectly.'

Merrilee stuck her whole head in.

'But it's empty,' she said in disbelief.

'If the missing part of the Book isn't here,' Gryla said, a horrible realisation crashing down on her, 'then where do we go next?'

'Oi!' came a shout. 'What are you doing?'

'We're delivering turkey-flavoured candy canes of course,' Merrilee said, not missing a beat. 'And I must say for such a fine establishment, you really do have messy storage facilities. We will have to think twice about supplying you with our world-renowned candy canes in the future unless you sort this mess out!'

And with that she dragged Gryla back upstairs.

'That was close,' Gryla said as they emerged back in the restaurant and tried to act casually.

A queue of people had formed outside, ready for the lunch rush. The place was already packed to bursting.

'Let's get out of here,' Gryla said, pushing past a table of young children bouncing about excitedly in their seats.

As they passed, one little boy in a festive jumper decorated with jingling bells leaned over and gave his grandmother a kiss on the cheek.

'NO KISSING WITHOUT MISTLETOE!' came a bellow, and the room fell silent.

A Krampus shot through the door and climbed on to the boy's end of the table.

The boy began to shake, his jumper playing a timid jingle.

Gryla watched in horror as the Krampus began

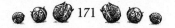

rifling around in the boy's backpack, in search of something to take as punishment. It growled and threw the backpack across the room, making everyone jump. Then it licked its lips and turned on the boy's grandmother.

'What is it doing?' Gryla whispered.

'NO!' the boy cried, but it was too late. The horrible beast hooked an arm around his grandmother's neck and dragged her outside.

The boy began to wail.

Gryla knelt down to comfort him, forgetting she was in a large turkey costume. 'I'll get her back,' she said. 'I promise.'

'That's them!' came a shout, and Gryla saw the waiter who'd caught them in the storeroom pointing madly in their direction.

'Run!' Merrilee shouted.

When they got to the bridge with the view of the Krampuses' lair, they stopped. They saw the Krampus flying over the river with the boy's grandmother and disappearing down a chimney. Seconds later, new Krampuses shot out.

'Shift change,' Merrilee said. 'What do we do now?'

Gryla gritted her teeth, her eyes on the lair. 'We go in.'

Chapter 24
The Krampus Lair

Two giant turkeys scuttled over the bridge to the Krampus lair and scaled a chimney.

'Down we go,' Merrilee said. 'Like proper Santas.'

All Gryla could feel was jagged rock. Its surface was covered in chalky soot that made her fingers itch.

Above them, the slit of light from the chimney's opening grew smaller and smaller and Gryla's breaths grew shorter. It felt as if they were descending to another planet – the air was thick with coal dust and choking them.

But they couldn't let the Krampuses hear them coming.

When Gryla heard a small crunch and the sound of boots on rock, she knew Merrilee had reached the bottom. Through the darkness she saw a hand reach out to help her down.

Finally the pair of them stood hunched in the opening of the fireplace, taking in the vast lair. Gryla couldn't believe her eyes. There were fireplaces every-where – exits to Humbug above. And all around them, clinging to every rock, limbs splayed and fast asleep, were Krampuses. Their eyes were closed and their snores rang out in bone-shaking growls.

Littering every surface were confiscated items. Thousands of them. Possessions stolen for bad festive behaviour – everything from toys and trinkets to sleighs.

'Let's look for that boy's grandmother and get out of here,' Gryla whispered.

They crept across the jagged rocks, ducking for cover every time they heard a rustle. The Krampuses were everywhere. It would be a disaster if they woke one up.

CRUNCH.

Gryla had stepped on an old toy car. Slowly she looked up, and there, right above her head, a Krampus snapped its eyes open!

She dived to the ground, lying as still as she could. She could see Merrilee just up ahead, bent low, her arms spread wide for balance, afraid to move an inch.

The Krampus grunted and shifted, shaking rocks loose on to Gryla's back. She tried not to move. The Krampus wriggled some more, until she was almost buried under rocks and dirt. Then she felt a *bang* as the Krampus hit the ground next to her. She held her breath.

Much to her relief, the monster stalked off further down the lair.

'I think he just couldn't get comfy,' Gryla whispered.

They carried on searching through the vast lair. There was all sorts down there: precious jewellery, holographic elves and out-of-season shoes.

'I don't think the grandmother is here,' Merrilee whispered.

'Haven't you found what you're looking for yet?' came a voice from the shadows.

It was a voice that made Gryla's blood run cold.

Slowly, they turned to see Klaus emerging from the shadows in his jolly red suit. Next to him was the grand-mother from the Christmas Lunch Club.

'I knew you wouldn't be able to resist trying to rescue an innocent person,' he mocked. 'Does she remind you of your grandmother, Gryla?'

'How do you know about my grandmother?' Panic was rising in Gryla's voice as she and Merrilee stepped out of the silly turkey costumes to face Klaus.

'Oh, I've been getting to know her very well,' he said, 'but you don't need to worry about that now.'

With a click of his fingers, all the Krampuses' eyes snapped open.

A moment later, they pounced!

Gryla felt herself being crushed against the floor.

Then everything went dark.

Chapter 25

Dungeons

When Gryla came round, she found herself in the palace dungeons, with Tinselcat, Merrilee's dad, Merrilee and Fred, her holographic elf.

There was no sign of the Book.

'I need to make a toy now, Merrilee,' Fred was saying.

'FRED,' Merrilee said firmly. 'It is not the time. I'm a prisoner in a dungeon, for Christmas's sake!'

'What better time to catch up on requesting a toy! What better things have you got to do? Present time! Present time! Present time! Present time! Present time!'

'Oh please just request something so he goes away,' Merrilee's dad begged. His fancy red suit was gone now, replaced with an old, soot-covered shirt and trousers with holes in the knees. He sat close to Merrilee, his hand on hers. Even without the outfit, Gryla still found she thought of him as Santa. A harmless, quite nice one.

'Fine,' Merrilee said. 'I would like an ice chimney obstacle course, please, Fred.'

Fred scrunched up his face.

Nothing.

He tried again.

Nothing.

'Oh,' he said. 'You're in the dungeons, so you're not allowed presents in here. We'll try again if you ever get out alive.'

'Thank you, Fred,' Merrilee said faintly, and with a *pop* he was gone.

'You know,' Tinselcat said, 'I'm starting to really like Fred.'

'I hope they haven't broken into my office,' the former Santa said, as he stared through the bars.

'They definitely will have,' Merrilee said.

'But it's password protected,' he said.

Merrilee stared at him. 'And is your password something very guessable, like HoHoHo?'

'Erm, no,' her dad said sheepishly.

'Oh look!' Merrilee said. 'Gryla's awake.'

Gryla got to her feet. 'Merrilee, we have to get out of here,' she said, racing to the bars. She rattled them as hard as she could, but they wouldn't budge. 'Klaus has my book, and the Carols will be here soon to finish Operation Bring Down Santa.'

The former Santa gasped.

'Not you, the other Santa,' Gryla said. 'But they can't do it if I haven't got the Book and the rest of the Brussels Sprout Brew recipe.'

'I have no idea what to do,' Merrilee said.

'What are you two plotting?' her dad asked.

Merrilee smiled. 'Together with the elves, we're

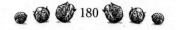

going to destroy the Krampuses and the weird Christmas world.'

'WHAT?' he cried. 'Oh, not this again. You're going to get yourself killed.'

'I won't,' Merrilee said. 'I've got a witch on my side.'

'A WITCH?!' he screamed.

'We'll bring back Christmas once a year and a Santa who delivers presents via chimneys.'

Her dad put his head in his hands. 'You're just like your mother.'

Merrilee grinned. 'You could retire and enjoy your days without a Krampus watching your every move. You could stop saying ho ho ho!'

'Oh,' the former Santa said sadly.

'Or you could keep saying it, I know that's your favourite bit,' Merrilee said.

'I hate to tell you girls,' he said, 'but the elves aren't real any more. They're extinct.'

'I promise you they're not,' Merrilee said.

'Shall we sing a song to raise our spirits?' he said,

trying to steer Merrilee away from the dangerous plan.

> *Oh Christmas tree, oh Christmas tree!*
> *Decorate it or ... KRAMPUS!*
> *Oh Christmas tree, oh Christmas tree,*
> *How lovely is ... the KRAMPUS.*

'RIGHT, CELL FIVE, EVERYONE OUT,' came a shout from a Snowman, his suit shedding snowflakes as he fiddled with the lock. 'Time to go.'

'Where are you taking us?' Gryla asked.

'To the witches,' he said.

Gryla froze. 'W-witches?'

He fixed her with a stare. 'They're all here. Now he just needs you.'

Chapter 26

Witches

The Snowman led them to the palace courtyard, where Gryla's whole coven were standing, hemmed in by an intimidating circle of gnashing Krampuses.

'Gryla!' came a cry, and her grandmother tried to rush to her.

'CONTROL THE WITCHES!' Klaus shouted, and a Krampus forced her back.

All around the courtyard a crowd had gathered. They looked furious, their eyes wild, their fists waving.

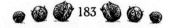

'They eat children!'

'They want to wipe out Christmas!'

'MONSTERS!'

Gryla was completely overwhelmed. She wanted to be back in the caves on the Mince Pie Isles where life was simple and people were kind.

'Gryla,' her grandmother called out sadly. 'Come to us.'

Gryla raced over, Tinselcat tucked tightly under her arm.

Klaus bellowed a sinister 'HO, HO, HO! Look at that witch – running to join her abominable friends!'

He nodded to a Snowman, who grabbed hold of Merrilee and her dad.

'You'll have a nice view of the witches' demise from that tower up there,' he said.

'Gryla!' Merrilee cried as she was dragged away.

'I'm so sorry,' Gryla said. 'I've ruined everything!'

'Sssh,' her grandmother said, holding her tight. 'It could have happened to anyone.'

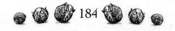

'What is he doing?' Cackle asked, trying to see past the Krampuses.

'This book …' Klaus began.

'Oh no, he has your book, Gryla,' Tinselcat said with a wince.

'… has protected witches for thousands of years. But if the Book is destroyed, we will also destroy the witches.'

He pulled at a rope and a fireplace with a little chimney breast dropped into the courtyard with a *bang*. A fire began roaring in its hearth.

'I thought it was fitting,' he said.

'He won't …' Tinselcat said with a gasp, just as the horrible new Santa threw the Book into the fire!

'NO!' Gryla screamed.

The reflection of the flames flickered in the witches' eyes as they watched the Book crisp and curl.

'BURN, WITCHES!' Klaus cried as the Book disintegrated into nothingness.

Klaus checked the fire embers and then counted the witches.

'It's gone,' Gryla said, a tear snaking down her face. 'The Book is gone.'

'But … we're still here,' Cackle said.

Klaus checked the fire for a second time and counted the witches again.

'WHY AREN'T THEY VANISHING WITH THE BOOK?'

'We should be dead,' Gryla's grandmother whispered.

'What's gone wrong?' Cackle said. 'Or should I say *right.*'

Gryla screamed, making everyone jolt, including the Krampuses.

'Oh good,' Klaus said, 'it's finally working!'

The crowd began whispering and jostling to get a better look.

'Are you all right?' her grandmother said. 'Why the screaming?'

'I know why it didn't work!' Gryla whispered excitedly. 'There's a bit of a page missing in the Book. A half spell. I wondered why someone would do that – and now I know! Whoever did it, they did it to protect us. As

186

long as the *whole* Book isn't burned, no one can destroy us!'

Gryla gasped again.

'But none of us did that,' her grandmother said. 'No witch would tear the Book. We wouldn't have dared!'

The other witches mumbled in agreement.

'Well, someone dared,' Gryla said.

'Who?' Cackle asked.

Gryla slumped. 'I don't know.'

'This is getting embarrassing,' Klaus said, kicking the embers of the fire. 'Let's just do it ourselves.' He raised a hand to command the Krampuses and their jaws opened.

Gryla heard someone whistle.

The Krampuses advanced. Then came a jingle.

Everyone stopped and looked up just as Merrilee's sleigh *whooshed* overhead.

Merrilee was hanging out of her prison tower, whistling as loudly as she could.

'THAT'S IT, RUDOLPHS!' she cheered, leaping from the tower into her trusty sleigh and knocking

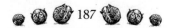

down Krampuses like skittles.

'TINSELBROOMS!' a witch roared, shooting across the courtyard to where the witches' confiscated cloaks and brooms were piled high.

'YOU SEE WHAT THE WITCHES ARE!' Klaus roared, whipping the crowd into a frenzy. 'KRAMPUSES, ATTACK!'

Soon Gryla was the only one left on the ground. The only one except for the angry mob, that is.

'Oh no,' she whispered.

'GET THAT WITCH!' they cried.

'Gryla,' Tinselcat said. 'RUN LIKE YOU HAVE NEVER RUN BEFORE!'

She slipped and skidded across the icy ground, and then felt her stomach lurch as she went flying forward, landing flat on her face. She felt a puff of air at her neck, followed by a hand on her collar.

For a second she thought it was all over.

'Well, at least you're finally free of the Book, eh?' Merrilee said.

Chapter 27

A Very Festive Fight

The battle was intensifying. High up on the snowy peak where the palace sat, Humbug people in their festive jumpers threw candy canes at witches on twinkling tinselbrooms, while Krampuses, fangs bared, snapped and snatched every witch they could.

Klaus had retreated to the palace.

'This is getting out of hand,' Merrilee said. 'Gryla, we're running out of time. If the Carols arrive to *this*, it will be no good – LOOK OUT!'

Gryla turned to see a Krampus hurtling towards her.

She ducked as Merilee swerved the sleigh.

'That was close,' Tinselcat said. 'I might just … oh yes … urgent appointment for me under this sleigh seat here …'

Gryla sat in the back, her mind racing as she watched witches tear through the sky above them.

'I'll keep us safe while you just *think*,' Merrilee said. 'We need another plan.'

Gryla was thinking hard about the missing bit of the Book. 'Wait a minute,' she said, getting to her feet and nearly being knocked straight off them again by a flying Krampus.

'What?' Merrilee asked excitedly. 'What is it?'

'Well,' Gryla said slowly, 'the person who tore the recipe wasn't a witch but must've liked witches enough to want to protect them. And they would have to know a lot about magic. They'd have to know about the Book in the first place, then they'd have to know that ripping out a bit of it would stop its destruction from in turn wiping out the witches. It seems not even witches knew that was possible …'

'Who would know more about your own magic than you?' Merrilee said.

Gryla's eyes grew wide. 'A CAROL!'

'You think an elf did it? But—'

'Merrilee!' Gryla screeched as a herd of Krampuses came charging.

'Hang on,' Merrilee said, swivelling the sleigh to see another herd charging from the other direction.

Merrilee raised the reins.

The Krampuses were almost upon them when –

WHOOSH! Merrilee sent the reindeer shooting upwards.

Gryla leaned over the edge to see the herds of Krampuses colliding with a *crunch*.

'Sorry,' Merrilee said. 'You were saying.'

'It has to be an elf who did it.'

'But why didn't they just say?' Merrilee said. 'We were right there with them when we discovered the Book had been torn. Why wouldn't they mention it was them? They seemed as shocked as us. Plus, they live for thousands and thousands of years, so the elf who did it – even if it was ages ago – would still be alive.'

Gryla gasped. 'There's one elf that did die! The Carol whose magic was used to make the Krampuses!' All the pieces started to fall into place in Gryla's mind. 'She saw the creation of the Krampuses and knew that they would want to eliminate the witches – magical beings who would preserve the old idea of Christmas. It makes sense!'

'Gryla, you're a genius!' Merrilee cried.

Gryla's eyes grew wide again as another memory came flooding back. It was the memory of the old woman on the shore who had given her Tinselcat.

He won't ever tangle, or tell.

'It's a shame Carol's not alive so we could ask her where she hid the rest of the recipe,' Merrilee said glumly.

'We don't have to,' Gryla said. 'I know where it is!'

Chapter 28

Fred

Merrilee landed the sleigh in a clearing at the gates of the palace and summoned Fred.

'You want an electric razor?' Fred said, puzzled.

'Yes, I would like it … as a … toy,' Merrilee said casually, ducking to avoid a stray candy cane hurtling her way.

'And as quickly as possible, please, Fred?' Gryla added.

'I'm not sure an electric razor is a toy, it's not coming up in my Toy Database. But OK! Let's do this – a toy request, HOORAY!'

 193

'Just a very quick electric razor,' Merrilee said. 'We're in a battle, Fred.'

A witch swooped low and flew right through Fred, making him shudder.

'Now, there are hundreds to choose from. Oh this is exciting! The SantaClipper is best in range?'

'Any old fast electric one,' Gryla said.

'Very well.' Fred squeezed his eyes shut and with a *bang* he produced a shiny new electric razor.

'Brilliant!' Gryla said, grabbing it.

'And it wasn't even for you, Merrilee!' Fred shouted, throwing his hands in the air. 'Can't even count that against my targets,' he groaned.

Gryla coaxed Tinselcat out from where he was hiding under the sleigh seat.

'Tinselcat, I need a small favour …'

Bzzzzzz.

'Gryla …' Tinselcat said.

Bzzzzzz.

'ARE YOU … ?'

Bzzzzzzz.

'YOU'RE SHAVING ME!' he roared as tinsel wafted around them.

'I just need to check something,' she said.

As the last strand of tinsel floated from Tinselcat and landed in the snow, something magical began to happen.

The pile of tinsel shavings rustled and sparked. Then a ghostly, glowing elf rose out of it holding a torn piece of paper.

'Oooh,' said a voice, and Gryla turned to see Fred behind her. 'What brand of elf is *that* – is it from the Rapid Elf range or the Gift-me-Elf range?'

'I'm a real elf,' the elf from the tinsel said. 'Well, the ghost of one.' She turned to Gryla. 'Who *is* this guy?'

'You're Carol!' Gryla said. 'The elf who died to make the Krampuses!'

'Oh great, is that my legacy?' Carol said with an eye roll. 'What year is it?'

 195

'It's 4029,' Gryla said.

'WHAT?' Carol cried. 'YOU'VE TAKEN ABSO-
LUTELY AGES TO SORT THIS MESS OUT. I DIED
EONS AGO! Here, you'd better have this.'

She handed Gryla the torn piece of paper she was
holding.

'The missing page,' Gryla whispered in amazement.

Carol nodded. 'I tore a page, with the permission of
Befana. It was her idea really – she came to me and told
me it would work. We knew without the complete Book,
no one could destroy the witches until they found it.
I made Tinselcat and hid the page within his fur. As
long as the witches lived, the true magic of Christmas
would live on too. I had witnessed the creation of the
Krampus Alliance. I had to do everything I could to
stop them. All I wanted was to keep the magic of
Christmas alive. And maybe bring *real* Santa, the toy-
making and all the joy back to the North Pole too, for
my elf friends.'

She looked around at the chaos. 'It's going well, is it?'

'It is now,' Gryla said, staring down at the missing part of the recipe. 'We have a plan.'

'Thank you for freeing me,' Carol said. 'I put my last drop of magic into Tinselcat, and when I died my spirit was bound to him.'

'IT'S FREEZING!' the now bald Tinselcat screeched.

Gryla picked him up and held him close.

'You know,' Gryla said to Carol, 'if Eggnog hadn't told me you'd made Tinselcat, I don't think I would've figured it all out.'

'Eggnog?' Carol said, her voice breaking. 'How is he? Is he OK?'

Gryla nodded. 'He's wonderful! He has a big family now.'

'Really?' Carol whispered.

'Really,' Gryla said. 'There are *loads* of them. And they all adore him.'

A tear rolled down Carol's cheek. 'Look after him for me.'

Behind Carol, a cloaked figure appeared out of thin air. When she pulled back her hood, Gryla recognised her instantly as the old woman who had given her Tinselcat!

'What's her name?' Gryla asked.

'Her?' the elf said, gesturing in the old lady's direction. 'That's the spirit of Befana.'

Carol turned to leave, her glow beginning to fade.

'Remember, you have the spell – use it now, before it's too late.'

'I will, I promise,' Gryla said as she watched them both disappear.

'GRYLA!' Merrilee screamed, her cheeks stained with tears. She pointed high up to the palace.

There, sitting on an ornate and very large Christmas pudding carved on the very tallest tower was her dad.

Behind him stood Klaus.

'DON'T!' Merrilee shouted, just as Klaus gave the former Santa a push.

Chapter 29

Cackle

Merrilee charged to her sleigh, but her dad had vanished from sight before she reached it.

She collapsed in a sobbing heap.

From high up in the palace, Klaus laughed.

'I don't know why he's laughing,' came a shout, and Cackle came flying through the air on her broom – with a familiar Santa-shaped lump clinging to the back.

'DAD!' Merrilee cried.

'Imagine thinking the best thing to do was to push him from a height, when down below is a bunch of

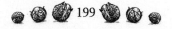

flying witches!' Cackle scoffed as she landed with a thud.

'He didn't think the witches would save Santa,' Gryla said with a smirk. 'Underestimating us, as always.'

'Thank you, Cackle,' Merrilee's dad said. 'You saved my life.'

The Humbug folk stopped fighting.

'That witch just saved Santa!'

'No!' Klaus shouted. 'I'M SANTA NOW!'

'The witch is a hero!' cried another.

'I think witches are maybe … good?' said another.

'FINE,' Klaus said. 'IF YOU MUST BE LIKE THAT THEN IT'S THE KRAMPUS JAWS FOR ALL OF YOU!'

'He's really lost it,' Merrilee said.

Gryla looked at the clock. They only had ten minutes until the Krampus shift change. She had to make the potion.

'I've got the recipe,' she said, making Merrilee yelp with delight. 'But I need to brew it.'

'Go!' Merrilee cried. 'We'll fight off the Krampuses here.'

Gryla charged off. When she reached the bridge that led to the Krampuses' lair, she screeched to a halt.

She knew the perfect place to brew the potion and she knew how to get there. She ran as fast as she could, all the way to the Christmas Lunch Club.

Inside the store cupboard, Gryla plucked candy canes off the wall and then ran to the kitchen for a pot to melt them in. She thought of Uma Garland brewing it down there in the basement all those years ago and got to work.

The ingredients and recipe were clear in her head. She stewed and squashed the Brussels sprout-flavoured candy canes, before adding a yuletide bouquet of cinnamon, clove, nutmeg and sage flavours.

Next came cherry flavour, and then a sprinkle of shaved fig flavour, which turned the mixture black. An egg-flavoured candy cane, a clump of dust from the floor and a kiss finished it off.

'Bleurgh.'

Finally Gryla gave it a quick stir, which turned it putrid green. It began to bubble.

With the pot in her arms, Gryla raced over the bridge to the Krampuses' lair, the Brussels Sprout Brew sloshing as she ran. Behind her, the palace was swarming with witches and Krampuses battling it out in the skies.

She scurried over to the first chimney she saw, her boots slipping on the loose rocks. Then she took a deep breath, and tipped the potion in.

It glowed a bright green as it snaked down the cracks in the chimney and into the lair.

She waited.

Silence fell below ground.

And then came the thuds and snores as the potion took hold.

She'd done it!

Now she just had to wait for the Carols.

Snow was falling thick and fast, the sky one big

smudge. The palace was disappearing too, blotted out by a curtain of white.

The Carols had to be in the lair before the other Krampuses returned for shift change. There were only seconds left.

Like magic, the sound of jingling bells filled the air.

Gryla looked up and saw the most beautiful sleigh she had ever seen soaring overhead. It was painted a rich, shiny red and lined with gold. And the best bit was the reindeer – there were nine of them, decked out in fur-trim harnesses and antler bells.

Piled high in the sleigh were the Carols.

'Sorry we're a bit late!' Inventor Carol shouted down. 'Someone wanted to stop halfway for a toilet break, and then the waitress insisted on taking photos with each of us – *individually*!'

They landed with a bump and leaped out, smiling at Gryla before they dived down the chimneys. There wasn't a moment to lose.

'We'll use our magic to overpower and undo what

Carol's magic did before,' Inventor Carol explained. 'I'd stand back if I were you, I'm not sure how it affects anyone who isn't an elf. Keep the non-magical folk away.'

And off he went down the chimney to join the others.

'It's shift change!' Merrilee cried as she flew up fast in her sleigh. 'Are the elves here? Is everything in place?'

Right on cue, the Krampuses flew overhead, back to their lair for shift change. What they didn't know was that they'd find their friends asleep, and a horde of elves to greet them. One after another, they disappeared down the chimneys into the depths of the lair, until they were all gone.

Gryla stepped back from the chimneys. 'That's it! Everything is in place,' she said with a grin. 'All ready to—'

She froze.

Huge jaws emerged from the white fog, right behind Merrilee's head.

One last Krampus on his way to the lair.

In one quick snap, the Krampus snatched Merrilee from her sleigh and disappeared down the chimney with her.

'NO!' Gryla cried. 'HUMANS CAN'T BE IN THERE NOW. CAROLS, STOP! MERRILEE'S DOWN THERE!'

But it was no good.

The ground had already begun to shake. The chimneys were crumbling. Gryla tumbled backwards as bright technicolour lights shot out of every crack and chimney pot. They lit up the sky before raining down like wild snow.

Gryla was covered, her skin glistening.

Up at the palace the witches dropped from their brooms and stared at the strange and searing light.

The snowy peak on which the palace was built began to melt. Droplet after droplet formed, until there was water cascading down its surface. Huge chunks of ice began to fall away and the gingerbread walls of the palace began to crumble.

 205

One by one the Carols sprang out of the lair and landed back in their sleigh.

They were jumping and cheering and hugging each other.

'WHAT IS HAPPENING?' Klaus yelled, appearing on a balcony of the crumbling palace. 'WHERE ARE MY KRAMPUSES?'

'THEY'VE BEEN UNDONE! DON'T EVER USE OUR MAGIC TO MAKE EVIL KRAMPUSES AGAIN!' a Carol shouted up to Klaus.

'ELVES?!' Klaus cried in disbelief.

'WE'RE ALL CALLED CAROL!' Inventor Carol yelled.

The rumbles grew louder. The palace began to shake.

One by one, its gingerbread walls fell in until only Klaus's turret remained.

For a moment it seemed as if it might withstand the magic.

But with one small *crack* it crumbled like the rest, taking Klaus with it.

 206

* * *

As the elf magic continued to do its work in Humbug, bauble houses popped and were replaced with pretty townhouses, sleigh-flying signs fell from the sky as birds rose up and spread their wings. The ice melted and flowers bloomed.

Gryla hardly noticed the changes though. She knelt down next to what remained of the lair. 'Did anyone see Merrilee?' she asked.

'No,' the Carols said at once. 'She wasn't *in* there, was she?'

Gryla began sobbing.

'Woah,' came a voice. A head had popped out from the remains of one of the chimneys. 'Now *that* was a challenging chimney,' Merrilee said.

'Merrilee!' Gryla cheered, just as her friend slumped over and began snoring.

'My potion,' Gryla said proudly to the elves. 'Hopefully it'll wear off soon.'

Chapter 30

Christmas Melts Away

Gryla floated in the Carols' sleigh high above Humbug watching Christmas melt away, until next year.

Below she could see the coven gathering together. Her grandmother was there and everyone was congratulating Cackle on her speedy flying to save Merrilee's dad.

Merrilee snorted and jumped to her feet.

'What happened? Why was I asleep? Did we do it?'

Gryla smiled. 'Look,' she said.

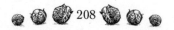

Merrilee peered down at a Humbug that was almost unrecognisable to her.

She had tears in her eyes. 'Finally,' she said.

'You did it,' Gryla said. 'I bet your mum would be so proud.'

'*We* did it,' Merrilee said, putting her arm around her friend's shoulder.

'Good old Christmas is back,' Gryla said. 'But who will be Santa?'

ALMOST A YEAR LATER

Chapter 31

Mince-Pie Picnic

Gryla soared through the sky on her broom, with a frozen Tinselcat hanging off the back.

They skidded to a stop, Gryla's boots ploughing through the snow before hitting a small and familiar candy cane.

It rose up out of the ground like a periscope.

'I'M SORRY,' came a little voice. 'THIS CANDY CANE CAN'T ANSWER YOUR CALL RIGHT NOW. PLEASE LEAVE A MESSAGE AFTER THE BEEP. *BOOOOING.*'

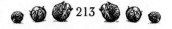

'NO, THAT'S NOT RIGHT,' another voice said. 'A BEEP IS JUST *BEEEEEP*.'

Gryla laughed.

'Oh,' the voices said at once. 'It's Gryla!'

There was a click and the world began to spin, whipping the snow into a tornado. Gryla was lifted into the air as the North Pole twisted and turned around her.

She felt her boots hit the ground and Carolburg came into view. What had been a neglected town a year ago was now alive with activity. Carols were rushing everywhere, carrying huge sacks of presents. The whole place had been cleaned up and was shining like new.

And some new residents had moved in.

'We do a cheers like this,' a Carol said, clinking his tiny mug against the Krampus's gigantic one.

The Krampus grinned – its awful fangs had been replaced with large, blunt teeth.

The elves had used their magic to transform the

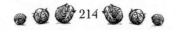

Krampuses and transport them to the North Pole. They'd made a few creative adjustments, like the teeth. And the Krampuses had hoofs instead of claws. Much safer.

Over by the ice rink, Krampuses skated happily. Others were helping to feed and brush the reindeer, and another was loading presents into the sleigh.

'LAST-MINUTE TOY TRAIN REQUEST. CAROL, WHERE ARE YOU? I NEED WHEELS!'

'HAS ANYONE SEEN PRANCER'S ANTLER BELLS?'

Gryla smiled.

Christmas felt magic again.

The whole world felt magic again.

There was excitement in the air.

She wandered into the workshop and stood to admire the place.

'I think you might want to see this letter,' Inventor Carol said.

Dear Santa

I've not been very good. In fact I've been power hungry. Anyway, I'd love a new bike. Now that it's not snowing all the time, I think I'd enjoy riding one.
    Sorry again.

Klaus the former Snowman (and power-hungry Santa)

Gryla smiled. 'What list did he end up on?' she asked.

'It's a pretty good apology, I suppose,' Inventor Carol said, and he pointed to a bike-shaped wrapped present.

'Good decision,' Gryla said.

'Carol!' came a shout.

'Yes?' all the Carols yelled back.

'It's confusing sometimes,' Inventor Carol said.

'Eggnog!' came another shout.

'Yes?' yelled all the trees.

'And confusing that all the trees are some form of Eggnog,' Inventor Carol added.

'Krampus!' came another shout.

'Yes?' grunted all the Krampuses.

'WHAT IS WRONG WITH US?!' Inventor Carol cried. 'THERE ARE HUNDREDS OF US AND ONLY THREE NAMES! Well, unless you count Fred.'

The holographic elf appeared with a *pop* next to him. 'You rang, Carol?'

Gryla strolled through the town, where technicolour icicles twinkled like they had done thousands of years before.

There was one other person there with a different name.

'Where's Santa?' Gryla asked.

'RIGHT HERE!' came a shout, and Merrilee popped out from a nearby ice chimney. 'Thought I'd get in one more practice before I fly.' She wiped the sweat from her brow with a holly-decorated hanky. 'I'm just going to

217

tidy myself up. Meet me back at Christmas Lodge in five minutes,' she said. 'I have something cool to show you.'

Christmas Lodge, where Merrilee lived with her dad, was the only not elf-sized house in town. Unless you counted the swish and very icy underground Krampus lair.

'GRYLA,' came a bellow, and she saw Eggnog bounding towards her, his Christmas ornaments jingling all over the place.

'Eggnog!' she said, running fast into his fir and giving him a huge hug. 'I have a little something for you.'

She pulled a small wrapped present from her cloak.

'I WILL SAVE IT UNTIL TOMORROW,' he said. 'THANK YOU.'

'Oh,' Gryla said, pulling another present from her cloak. 'No, *this* one is for Christmas Day, you can open the first one now.'

Eggnog gave an excited shake and ripped the parcel open. He held it up with his leafy branches to inspect it.

It was a small bowl decorated with Christmas trees.

'LOVELY,' Eggnog said, unsure what to do with it. 'AND JUST MY SIZE,' he lied.

'It actually comes with something else,' Gryla said, and she gently placed a frozen Tinselcat on one of his branches.

In the warmth of Eggnog he defrosted in seconds.

She gave him a tickle under the chin.

'It's a cat bowl, Eggnog,' Gryla explained. 'Tinselcat and I have been talking—'

'A lot,' Tinselcat interrupted.

'And we've decided he should come and live here – with you. He belongs in this festive place. Plus he was yours first. I think Carol would want you to have him.'

Eggnog enveloped Tinselcat in a warm, leafy hug as the cat purred.

'THANK YOU,' Eggnog tried to whisper, but it still came out loud enough to shake the snow off the workshop roof.

'And I can visit Tinselcat every year,' Gryla said, her words faltering. She knew it was the right thing to do, but her heart still felt heavy.

Merrilee appeared beside them in a smart red suit. 'It's nearly time,' she said. 'But first we're going to have a mince-pie picnic. Inventor Carol told me about them. He said the real Santa always used to have one before setting out to deliver the presents.'

So that Christmas Eve, Merrilee and Gryla set out a blanket on the snow and fetched some mugs of hot chocolate and a tray of mince pies. They lay down, staring up at the stars, and they ate their mince pies – every last one.

It was tradition, after all.

Epilogue

The two witches watching the bauble sat in their chairs, bored, looking at yet another blizzard.

'Why are they *still* making us watch it?' the red-haired witch complained.

'Because they think we're good at spotting stuff now,' the pink-haired one said. 'Bet we just see a blizzard. It's almost always just a blizzard.'

As if it had heard them, the blizzard in the bauble changed from white to bright orange shot through with

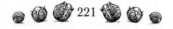

swirls of yellow. The colours began to swirl, faster and faster and faster, just like it had done before.

The witches rose from their chairs and hurried closer.

Inside, they could see the ghost of an elf, and an old woman, her eyes cloudy, frosted over like ice. She was wearing a black swimming costume and the elf a red-and-white-striped bikini.

They were lying on … lilos? The witchy-looking one was writing something.

'What are you writing?' the spirit of Carol asked.

'A new book,' the spirit of Befana replied.

'Anything good?'

'Not sure yet, it's got a lot of sprouts in it.'

'Lovely,' Carol said. She plucked the cocktail umbrella out of her drink and took a sip. 'I'd read it.'

'What are we watching?' the red-haired bauble witch whispered.

The pink-haired one shrugged. 'I think it might be … ghosts on holiday?'

And with that, Befana looked right at them, making them jump.

She winked.

And then the bauble burst into a million pieces.

Have you read

What if somewhere along the way we've all got the
Santa story a bit wrong … ?

A funny, festive sleigh ride you'll never forget!

Turn the page for a sneak peek …

Prologue

What do we know about 'Mrs' Claus? The truth is: *almost nothing*. She lives in the background of Christmas stories all around the world, and that is where we have kept her for hundreds of years. But what if, a long time ago, we got the story wrong? What if the truth disappeared out of sight, and she along with it?

It is a story she wanted people to know – a story of resilience and little acts of kindness. A story of *real* tinsel and how two formidable girls changed Christmas forever.

This is her story.

This is the story of Blanche Claus.

Chapter 1
The Bauble

Once upon a time – over one hundred years ago – there lived a girl with ice-white hair who truly hated Christmas.

The girl's name was Blanche Claus, and on this Christmas – the Christmas when we find her – everything seemed entirely ordinary at first. She was alone in London, huddled under the bridge she called home. Across the river, horse-drawn carriages danced along frozen streets, practically flying people to their destinations. She stared at the scene longingly. Everyone had somewhere to be on Christmas Day. Everyone except her.

Blanche, somewhat uniquely, spent her Christmases counting down the seconds until the day was over. Preferably as loudly as possible.

'Eighty-six thousand, three hundred and twenty-four! Eighty-six thousand, three hundred and twenty-three!'

Her parents had died before her memories began, and Blanche's life had been little more than a blizzard-blur of the city's orphanages, each one more ghastly than the last. But by the time she was four she was determined never to spend another night in an orphanage again. No matter where she was taken, she rarely stayed longer than an hour. Despite the bolted doors and barred windows, she always escaped.

How she escaped remained a mystery to everyone.

'Eighty-five thousand, one hundred and four! Eighty-five thousand, one hundred and three!'

She knew she wasn't one of the lucky ones – she was alone, and Christmas more than any other day of the year reminded her of that.

'EIGHTY-FOUR THOUSAND, EIGHT HUNDRED AND TWO! EIGHTY-FOUR THOUSAND, EIGHT HUNDRED AND ONE!'

Normally, the Christmas countdown would go on until the day was done or Blanche had fallen asleep, but this year was different. Something distracted her.

A cloaked old woman was hobbling in her direction.

Blanche halted her counting and waited for the woman to pass by, but she grew closer and closer until there was barely space for a snowflake between them.

A red bauble dangled from her finger.

'Hello?' Blanche whispered, her voice cracking like nervous ice.

The old woman pulled back her hood, revealing white hair just like Blanche's. Her eyes were cloudy, frosted over like the river. She leaned in closer.

'This is for you,' she rasped. And she held out the bauble for Blanche to take.

'For me?' Blanche asked, presuming a mistake had been made.

'For you,' the old woman insisted. 'For Christmas.'

'Thank you,' Blanche said quietly. 'I've never been given a Christmas present before. But … I should be honest – it'll be wasted on me. I don't have a tree to hang it on. You should keep it.'

'You don't need a tree for this bauble.'

'Then what will I do with it?' Blanche asked.

'Only you know that,' the old woman said mysteri-ously. 'Never underestimate the gifts you are given. What you see inside might surprise you.'

Blanche raised an eyebrow sceptically, but the old woman held the bauble closer. Carefully, Blanche lifted it by its gold thread and cupped it in her hands. She'd thought it must be a trick, but the bauble was impossibly cold. Colder than ice.

'Merry Christmas,' the old woman whispered with a smile, just as the red surface of the bauble began to swirl.

Blanche looked closer, peering past the shimmering streaks of festive colour to what lay beyond. She could see a snowy landscape decorated with tiny houses and technicolor icicles! And right in the middle was ... a giant dancing Christmas tree?

She blinked, convinced she was imagining it, but when she looked again it was still there. Its decorations clashed against each other as it twirled madly, making some of them fizz and shatter like fireworks.

'I-I-I can see—' she began, too excited to get the words out. 'It's—' She looked up at the old woman for answers.

But the old woman was gone.

Chapter 2
A Horse

The bauble was just the beginning.

After that, Blanche felt something change in her – a flurry of snow in her belly so strong she thought it might raise her up into the sky. Suddenly, it didn't seem right to spend the rest of Christmas Day under the bridge, counting down the seconds until it was over. The world inside the bauble had made her see that adventures were out there. The old woman had made her realise – if only for a second – that she wasn't truly alone. And the magic of holding on to one small thing that felt like it might just change everything was enough to make her stand up and start walking.

That day – that moment – changed Christmas for everyone.

With a new sense of hope, Blanche made her way across the bridge and into town. She walked past houses dressed for Christmas, with windows framing roaring fires and fat turkeys on tables. She had no destination in mind – she just walked. The empty streets were covered in fresh snow and she sighed happily. London felt like it was all hers. She had just started to dance, twirling through the silence and catching snowflakes on her tongue, when the most unexpected sight made her stop.

There was a horse standing alone in the middle of the road.

The poor thing looked abandoned, with her neck bent low and her ribs on show. She was shivering, so Blanche approached slowly, making a clicking noise, which she hoped the horse would interpret as friendly.

'It's all right,' she whispered, getting close enough to pat her neck. The horse flinched.

'Don't be scared,' Blanche said. She spotted a pile of empty sacks stacked on some barrels and began layering them on the horse's back for warmth. In one she found some old Christmas puddings and laid them out on the snowy ground for the horse to munch on.

'What's your name?' Blanche whispered, as if the horse might be able to answer. 'I can't just call you Horse.'

She waited a moment, then looked down at the writing on the sacks.

RUDY'S CHRISTMAS PUDDINGS.

'Rudy …' Blanche tried out loud.

The horse neighed enthusiastically.

'Rudy!' Blanche cheered, nestling her face into the horse's wispy mane. 'Well, now that I know your name, I should probably return you to your owner.'

She began to look around, but Rudy whinnied loudly and shook her head from side to side.

Blanche stared. It was as if Rudy had understood every word.

'You don't have an owner?'

Rudy whinnied again and an idea began to form in Blanche's head.

'Well, if you don't have an owner, then … would you like to come with me? I'll take care of you, always. I'll never leave you.'

Rudy nuzzled into Blanche and nibbled at the bauble sticking out of her pocket. Blanche took it as a sign.

'It's settled,' she said.

With an ear-splitting whinny, Rudy reared up, making Blanche leap back in fright! The horse began madly throwing her head up in the air as if trying to tell her something.

'What is it?' Blanche cried. 'What's wrong?'

Rudy spluttered impatiently and then tossed her head in the air again.

'Up?' Blanche said. She looked up to the sky.

Rudy stretched around and tapped her nose to her body.

'Oh, you want me to ride you? Is that it?' Blanche asked. 'I'm sorry, I can't. I don't know how to ride a horse.'

Rudy scraped her hoof on the ground and spluttered again.

'Don't be like that, it's not my fault,' Blanche said. 'I've never had the chance—'

Rudy interrupted her with another impatient splutter, then bit at Blanche's jacket, pulling her closer.

'OK, fine!' Blanche said. With an awkward leap, she half jumped, half heaved herself on to Rudy's back and fell forward, grabbing a tuft of the horse's mane.

She lay belly down for a second, scared to move. 'Now what?' she asked. 'Should I try sitting—?'

Rudy shot off through the London streets faster than Blanche had ever seen a horse move. She held on for dear life, wincing as they dodged lamp posts and crying out as they skidded around corners.

'RUDY!' she shouted. 'HALT! SLOW! STOP! FREEZE! WHAT IS HORSE FOR STOP?!'

Rudy neighed and Blanche was sure it sounded like a chuckle. She clung on, dangling by nothing but frozen fingers on a threadbare mane.

The whole world leaped around her in rocky jolts that made her feel sick. It was obvious Rudy had no intention of stopping, so Blanche took a deep breath and raised herself to a sitting position.

As soon as she did, the horse's heaving movements evened out and Blanche felt as if she and Rudy clicked into place.

'AM I HORSE RIDING? IS THIS IT?' Blanche cried. Rudy glanced back and winked.

They thundered on, and it wasn't long before Blanche began to enjoy herself. For the first time in years she was grinning from ear to ear.

'TALLY-HO!' she roared, just as something leaped into view, making Rudy rear up in fright. Before Blanche could do anything, the horse disappeared from under her and she tumbled backwards into the snow.

When she opened her eyes, slush blurred her vision. A watery outline of a figure swayed in front of her.

'LEAPING CHRISTMAS TREES! ARE YOU ALL RIGHT?!'

Chapter 3

The Corner Where Christmas Trees Are Sold

Two hands tucked under Blanche's armpits and hauled her upright. She hastily rubbed the snow out of her eyes, and the second surprising sight of the day came into focus.

It was a girl, around the same age as her, wearing the most unusual outfit Blanche had ever seen. The edge of her tattered skirt was trimmed with crumpled wrapping paper, and baubles hung from her ears. Her filthy jacket had a broken angel decoration stitched on to it like a brooch and her long dark hair was pulled into a plait wrapped with wilted mistletoe. It looked as though she'd been all over London picking up stray bits of Christmas.

'Your outfit,' Blanche said, 'is SPECTACULAR.'

The girl smiled and did a little bow. 'Why, thank you very much.'

'Where did you find all those things?' Blanche asked.

'Oh, on the street, mostly,' the girl said. 'Most of them were lost. That's why I wear them – so their owners can easily find them again!' She patted Rudy. 'I'm truly sorry for startling your horse. I LEAPED up and I don't think the horse expected it … I just got so excited when you came true.'

'When I what?' Blanche asked.

'Came true! You're my wish!' the girl said, hugging Blanche tightly. 'I didn't expect you to be delivered so quickly. Only seconds ago, I said to the snowy sky, "PLEASE CAN YOU SEND ME SOMEONE TO HAVE A MINCE-PIE PICNIC WITH?" And BOOM-SPLAT here you are! I think you're wonderful already and I've only known you for two seconds. I'm Rinki, and I would love you to join me for a mince-pie picnic.'

'Me?' Blanche managed, completely overwhelmed. She tucked her hand in her pocket to touch the ice-cold bauble again. 'I would love it,' she said quietly. 'I've never had anyone to spend Christmas with, and I've never been to a … um … what did you call it?'

'A mince-pie picnic!' Rinki cheered. 'It's only the best Christmas tradition *in the world*. I made it up myself, actually.'

She held out a handkerchief embroidered with candy canes and holly and peppered with holes, opening it slowly to reveal two slightly squashed mince pies with stale crusts.

'It's a feast!' she said. 'One each!'

They settled down in the snow and Rinki spread the small handkerchief out as if it were a sprawling picnic blanket.

'This street corner is where Christmas trees are sold,' she said. 'It's my favourite.'

Blanche stole a glance at the alleyway behind them, where Rinki had made a tent bed with an old blanket. She thought Rinki was probably alone this Christmas too.

'Such a lovely day for a mince-pie picnic! The most glorious weather, don't you agree?' Rinki said as she handed Blanche a mince pie. 'And it is pleasure to have you both here.'

She split her mince pie in two and fed one half to Rudy, then she raised the other half in the air like an adult would raise a glass to toast an occasion.

'To Christmas!' she cheered, shoving the mince pie in her mouth.

Blanche laughed. 'To Christmas!'

WITCH WARS

Read the whole ritzy,
glitzy, witchy series!

AVAILABLE NOW!

BAD Mermaids

SIBÉAL POUNDER

BAD Mermaids

Illustrated by Jason Cockcroft

SIBÉAL POUNDER

BAD Mermaids On the Rocks

Illustrated by Jason Cockcroft

Read the whole fabulously fishy series!

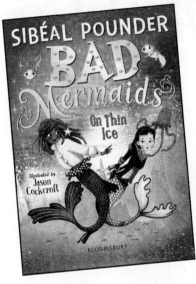

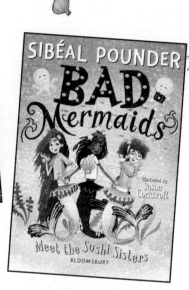

AVAILABLE NOW!

NEON'S SECRET UNIVERSE

Read the whole unicorn-tastic goo-powered series!

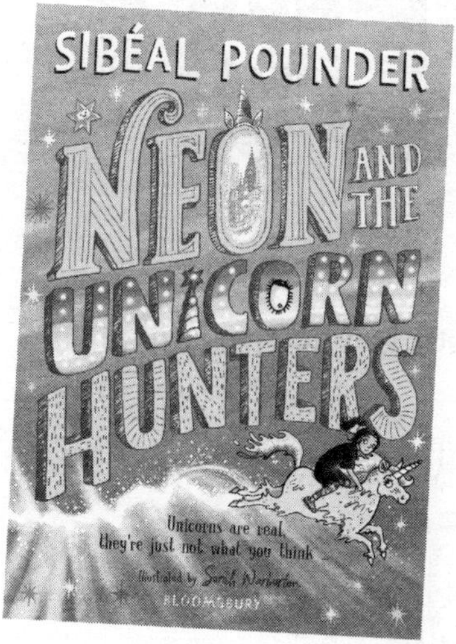
SIBÉAL POUNDER
NEON AND THE UNICORN HUNTERS
Unicorns are real, they're just not what you think
Illustrated by Sarah Warburton
BLOOMSBURY

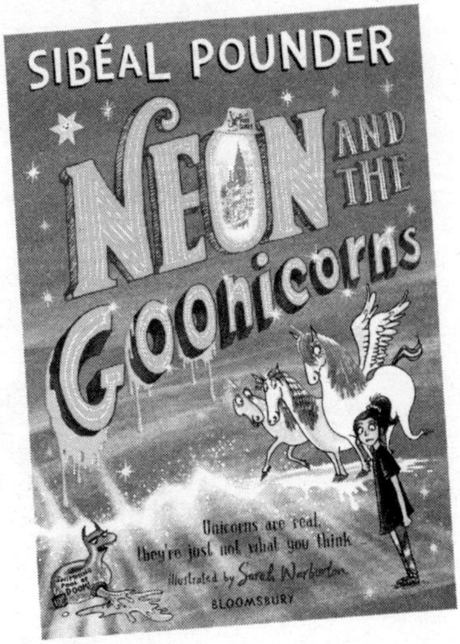
SIBÉAL POUNDER
NEON AND THE Goonicorns
Unicorns are real, they're just not what you think
Illustrated by Sarah Warburton
BLOOMSBURY

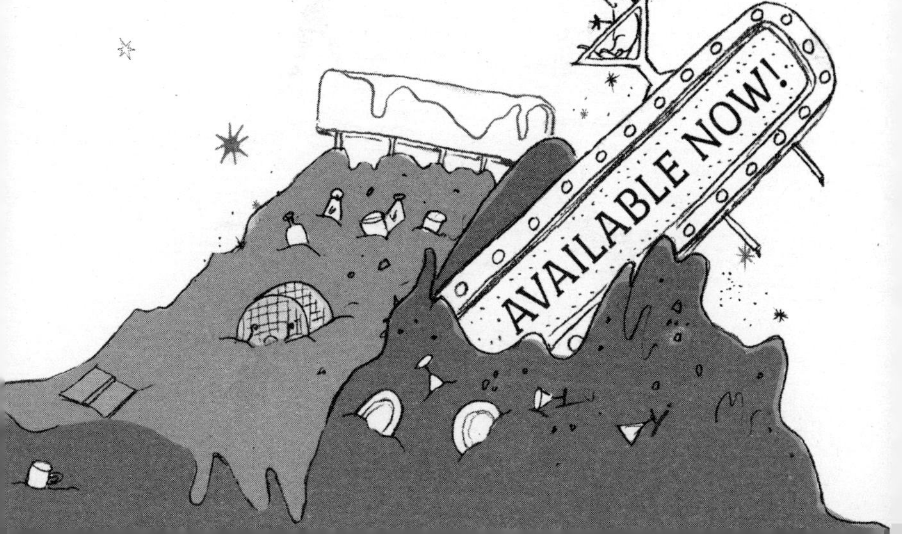
AVAILABLE NOW!

About [illegible]

Sibéal Pounder is a [illegible] author of the [illegible] series [illegible] Secret Diaries [illegible] She has also written Bea[illegible] The Secret of Platform 13 [illegible] novelisation of the [illegible] World [illegible] Book, Bad Mermaids [illegible] Waterstones Children's [illegible] Children's Book Award.

About the Author

Sibéal Pounder is a No.1 *New York Times* bestselling author of the much-loved and highly successful children's fiction series Witch Wars, Bad Mermaids and Neon's Secret UNIverse, and the Christmas hit, *Tinsel*. She has also written *Beyond Platform 13*, the sequel to *The Secret of Platform 13* by Eva Ibbotson, and the novelisation of the film *Wonka*. Her World Book Day book, *Bad Mermaids Meet the Witches*, was a *Sunday Times* bestseller, and *Witch Wars* was shortlisted for the Waterstones Children's Book Prize and the Sainsbury's Children's Book Award.

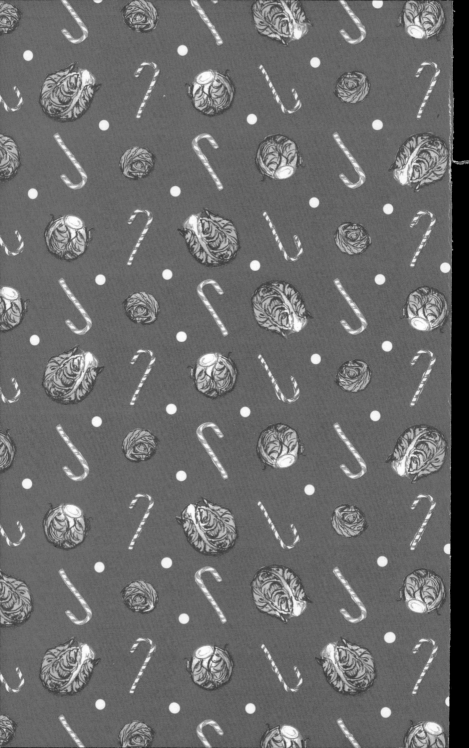